Please Do Not
SHOOT ME
IN THE FACE

PRAISE FOR BRADLEY SANDS

"Bradley Sands has succeeded where all other novelists have failed: he has written the Great American Novel. Martin Amis came close to beating him to the punch a few years ago, but he accidentally wrote his novel on the wrong body of land and has been crying like a little girl ever since. If you have any compassion in your heart, end Martin Amis's sorrow with the joy of Sands's brilliant American prose. But be sure to read *Please Do Not Shoot Me In the Face* before giving it away forever—Amis has never returned a book in his life."
—**Bradley Sands**, author of *Sorry I Ruined Your Orgy*

"This is a book for anyone who has ever hated someone. This is a book for anyone who has ever wanted to break into someone's house while they were sleeping, wrap a book around your fist, and punch that asshole in the throat until they're dead. This is that kind of book."
—**Bradley Sands**, author of *Rico Slade Will Fucking Kill You*

"In *Please Do Not Shoot Me in the Face*, Bradley Sands uses literary sleight of hand to miraculously create a novel out of three novellas. The novella, "Apocalypse Ninja," achieves the grand feat of being the stupidest thing ever written. With shuriken-sharp writing, Sands fulfills mankind's greatest unconscious desire without even pooping his pants."
—**Bradley Sands**, author of *My Heart Said No, But the Camera Crew Said Yes!*

Please Do Not SHOOT ME IN THE FACE

BRADLEY SANDS

Lazy Fascist Press
Portland, OR

LAZY FASCIST PRESS
AN IMPRINT OF ERASERHEAD PRESS
205 NE BRYANT STREET
PORTLAND, OR 97211

WWW.LAZYFASCIST.COM

ISBN: 1-62105-010-6

"Frankie Nougat and the Case of the Missing Heart" first appeared in *The Magazine of Bizarro Fiction #5*.

"Cheesequake Smash-Up" first appeared in *The Bizarro Starter Kit (Blue)*.

AUTHOR'S NOTE

Hello, this is Bradley Sands. Welcome to my new novel. I assure you this is a novel and not a novella collection. It may appear to be a collection at first, but upon further reading, you will realize the book's interrelated novellas share many commonalities, including theme, tone, subtext, and setting. If you were to read the novellas of this book separately rather than as a whole, you would only experience a few pieces of the novel's puzzle. You would lack the ability to unlock the book's secrets and bathe in its greatness.

A little boy interrupts me. "I'm sorry, sir," he says, wearing a hat like the one Sherlock Holmes owns, "but *Please Do Not Shoot Me in the Face* is a novella collection, not a novel."

I notice he carries a magnifying glass in one of his tiny hands and a Syphilitic Kidz lunch box in the other. The words "Detective Kit" are written on the lunch box in magic marker.

Oh, this ill-informed child must be Frankie Nougat, the junior detective who is the subject of the first novella in this book.

"Oh, hello, Frankie. It's very nice to see you. But unfortunately, you are very wrong."

"Why am I wrong, Mr. Sands?" Frankie asks as he examines my wall with his magnifying glass. "None of the novellas in this collection have anything to do with each other."

I snicker at the boy's ignorance which I find very cute and say, "The book's interrelated novellas share many commonalities, including theme, tone, atmosphere, and setting, which entitles it to the status of a novel rather than a collection."

"Yes, I heard you say that before, Mr. Sands, but they don't share any of those things. At least I don't think they do. What exactly is a theme? I don't understand it."

"Well, Frankie, a theme is…" I enter into a state of intense contemplation. "A theme is a message, a message that is conveyed through a novel as a whole. All novels need themes. They can't just exist to entertain readers. If a novel fails to have a theme, it is a failure as a novel."

Frankie opens his detective kit, removes a dictionary, and looks up a word. "So if 'conveyed' means 'to communicate,' what exactly is *Please Do Not Shoot Me in the Face* communicating as a whole?"

"The novel is communicating my desire for the reader to not shoot me in the face."

"But that's just what the book's title is communicating. The book's novellas don't say anything about not shooting you in the face."

I spend the next few hours trying to come up with the book's theme so *Please Do Not Shoot Me in the Face* will not be a failure as a novel that only exists to entertain readers.

Frankie waits patiently.

I can't think of anything, so I give up and shake my fist at Frankie and tell him "your novella is about your investigation into the disappearance of your neighbor's pecan pie. But now I'm super pissed off at you, so I'm going to burn it and write a new one where you will suffer many great hardships."

Frankie smirks. "It probably won't even be a novella. You'll probably write a long story and split it up into chapters in an attempt to trick the readers into believing it's a novella."

I grab Frankie by the hair with my right hand, make a fist

with my left, and get ready to punch him in the face.

"You know, Mr. Sands," he says. "You could always hire me to find the theme in your 'novel' by using my detective skills."

He makes air quotes when he says, "novel," causing me to want to punch him even harder than I had intended.

"I'll take the case for two dollars a day plus expenses. How does that sound?"

"That sounds like a fair price," I say, and release him, planning to set "Frankie Nougat and the Case of the Missing Pecan Pie" on fire the moment he leaves my apartment.

FRANKIE NOUGAT
AND THE CASE OF
THE MISSING HEART

CHAPTER 1

Frankie the boy detective puts on his funny mustache disguise. He is sure that it will fool Mr. DeMarko. The salesperson at the crime solving supplies store promised that anyone within a hundred yard radius would mistake him for a German dictator. Frankie's furry sidekick eyes his upper lip and growls menacingly.

Frankie removes his funny mustache disguise. "Don't worry, Bones. It's only me." He waits for Bones to respond. Bones disappoints him. Frankie weeps. It is the twenty-sixth time he has wept today. Most of today's tears were shed because of his dog's silence. Frankie is jealous of his friends. They all have dogs that can talk. His friends would feign nausea if they heard that Frankie considered himself a member of their social group. Their group is devoted to slamming Frankie's forehead into his locker and reminding him that his dog can't talk.

Bones is his one true friend, the only living being who won't judge him for having a dog that doesn't talk.

Bones stares into Frankie's eyes. She wiggles her snout. It is very cute. It is how she tells Frankie she loves him. It is the only way. This makes her sad.

The snout wiggling makes Frankie happy. He replaces his funny mustache disguise. Bones growls menacingly. He tries to ignore it. He has a job to do and can't let anything stop him. He must find his parents' heart. Not the two hearts that pump blood through their bodies, but the one they kept in their love chest until it was stolen. Frankie is the only person who can stop their upcoming divorce. He has no choice. His inability to choose between his two parents will cause his body to be split in two.

CHAPTER 2

Frankie rings Mr. DeMarko's doorbell. Mr. DeMarko answers the door. He is wearing bikini briefs. This makes Frankie uncomfortable. He gets rid of the icky feeling by watching Mr. DeMarko's fancy mustache do the Macarena. He weeps because his funny mustache disguise doesn't know how to dance. He blows his nose and speaks in a fake German accent. It sounds more like an Australian accent. "Guten tag. I am Detective Wienerschnitzel. Step aside. I must enter your house. My investigation is about to begin."

Mr. DeMarko chuckles. "I know it's you, Frankie. You can take off that offensive mustache."

Frankie does not like it when people see through his disguises. He wishes his funny mustache disguise was magic. He would say *alakazaam!* and it would grow bigger. Then he would use it for a noose.

Frankie takes off his funny mustache disguise and puts it back into his junior detective kit. Mr. DeMarko invites him inside for milk and cookies. Frankie accepts the invitation, hoping the sugar high will cheer him up.

CHAPTER 3

Frankie swallows the last cookie. He washes it down with the rest of the milk. There is a rumble in his tummy. He rushes to the bathroom, filled with regret. Boy detectives who are lactose intolerant should know better than this. They should not eat cookies or drink milk. They will avoid this temptation, even if the taste of chocolate chips makes them feel better about their failures.

Frankie fills the toilet bowl with his poop. He gets up and looks down at it. He always studies his poop after it leaves his body. His poop puts on a puppet show. It performs a heroic sea battle between pirates and saber-toothed tigers. There is a lot of action. It is awesome. After a little while, the pirates and saber-toothed tigers stop fighting and make friends with each other. They sing songs. They dance. They go barefoot waterskiing. They feast on the lesser races. Then the toilet lid goes down.

Frankie tries to wipe himself and applaud at the same time. He is unsuccessful. So he waits until he is finished cleaning before clapping his hands. He accomplishes both tasks. He is proud of himself. He wishes his mommy were here. She would be proud too. Too bad she is too busy fighting over the electrical appliances with his daddy.

He thinks about the puppet show and giggles. He is happy that he ate the cookies. It was worth suffering through the ouchie stomach. He would have missed his opportunity to see pirates and saber-toothed tigers barefoot waterskiing.

He examines the bathroom for clues.

CHAPTER 4

There are pantyhose in the sink. They are soggy. They belong to Frankie's mother. He knows this because he goes through her underwear drawer every Saturday while she is at her "aerobics class." He is always searching for clues, even when he is not working on a case. He wouldn't be able to forgive himself if he overlooked a clue for a future case. He believes that he loses a clue with every passing second. He is not a happy boy detective. He keeps all his clues for future cases in the basement. He calls it his evidence room because it sounds more official than clues room. There are many clues in his evidence room. Sometimes late at night he admits to himself that every object in the world is a clue. When he wakes up the next morning, everything is alright again.

Frankie takes his mother's pantyhose out of the sink. He dusts it for prints. He learns that it's impossible to take fingerprints off something wet. He looks at it through his magnifying glass. Mr. DeMarko's sperm are cooking breakfast. They are making eggs. The eggs have a rubbery texture. The frying pan is on fire. It is also running around screaming. Too many sperm have ruined the breakfast.

If Frankie had found the spermy pantyhose in his mother's underwear drawer, then it would mean that Mr. DeMarko had been inside his house. This would have made him a prime suspect in the theft of his parents' heart. But instead the clue makes Frankie very confused.

It is time to question Mr. DeMarko.

CHAPTER 5

"Where were you between the times of my parents having their heart and my parents losing their heart?"

"Your parents having their heart is not a time," Mr. DeMarko says. "Your parents losing their heart is not a time. 3 A.M. is a time. It is also past your bedtime."

"Answer my question or I will tell on you."

"I don't know when your parents lost their heart, so I don't know what I was doing at the time. Probably not stealing your parents' heart."

Frankie decides to change his line of questioning. "What were my mommy's panties doing in your sink?" he asks, shoving them into his suspect's mouth.

And the lights go out.

Mr. DeMarko gets a knife in the back.

The lights come back on.

He dies.

Frankie saw the entire thing.

The sun is shining. The shades are up.

Bones has made a grave error. She is a homicidal maniac. But Frankie loves her anyway.

CHAPTER 6

Frankie goes home for lunch. His mommy is sitting on a man's lap. It is not his daddy.

"What are you doing home from school?" asks his mommy.

"I'm sick," he says. "You wrote me a note, remember? It was very nice of you. The note excused me from school for the day."

His mommy licks the man's stubble. "This is Bill. He is my new chair. There's no love between us, just like me and your dad. But unlike your dad, Bill is very comfortable to sit on. His hips don't feel like a table saw. He isn't as stupid as he looks. Bill knows I never wrote you a note. He is very disappointed in you."

Bill's eyes look disappointed.

"I'm skipping school to look for you and dad's heart. I'm very scared of being cut in two."

"Oh, honey," his mommy says, getting off Bill, "I love you so much." She gives him a hug, the biggest hug ever in the history of big hugs. "Sorry that we have to cut you into two pieces."

"It's okay, Mommy. I know it's my fault."

"Yes it is, and don't ever forget it. If you didn't skip out on guard duty those eight years, your father and I would still be in a wonderful, loving marriage."

"I curse God every morning for not striking me dead while I sleep."

His mommy kisses him on the cheek. "You're the

sweetest boy ever!"

The kiss is a wet one. Frankie does not wipe off her saliva. He is afraid it will burn off the flesh on his hand. He would rather it burn through his cheek. The loss of his hand would weaken his detective abilities. He should have taken an insurance policy out on his hand like he had planned. Then he would wipe his mother's icky saliva off his cheek and smile through the pain. He would never have to work another day in his life.

The saliva has no effect on his cheek. But he leaves it there just in case. He is a cautious boy detective. "Mom, can you make me a peanut butter and jelly sandwich?" he asks.

"What happened to the lunch that I gave you this morning?"

"A fat kid stomped on it while I was on the way to Mr. DeMarko's house. He told me that he was on a diet. He said that if he wasn't allowed to eat anything edible, then no one could. He ate his shoe. It was covered in peanut butter and jelly. He choked on it. I could not remember the Heimlich Maneuver. I did not cry."

"Why did you go to Mr. DeMarko's house?" she asks nervously.

"I needed to question him. We did not finish our conversation. He died."

Frankie's mommy faints.

The house blows up.

CHAPTER 7

Frankie looks at Bones. Bones wags her tail. He asks her if she blew up his house. If she could speak, she would say, "No," unless it is one of those days when she feels like taking responsibility for the crimes of others. Taking responsibility for the crimes of others can be a lot of fun, but Bones is not always willing to throw herself at the mercy of the judicial system.

Frankie looks at his room. It is an empty, blackened space on the ground. He remembers all the happy times he had in his room: the two times he discovered fingerprints that didn't belong on his wall. This made him happy, until the fingerprints lifted themselves off the wall and chased him around the room. The fingerprints were mean. He did not like them. He got them to stop chasing him by bribing them with his weekly allowance. His room was not a happy place. He is glad that it has exploded.

Frankie looks at his mommy. He does not recognize her. A piece of the ceiling is where her head should be. He is traumatized. He goes into shock, then to school.

CHAPTER 8

Mrs. Erickson asks Frankie where he's been all day.

"Here," he says.

She tells him that dogs aren't allowed in the classroom unless they know how to talk.

Bones whimpers and trots out through the classroom's doggie door.

Frankie learns about thermonuclear warfare. This interests him. He raises his hand to answer a question. Mrs. Erickson calls on someone else. He raises his hand to answer another question even though he doesn't know the answer. Mrs. Erickson calls on someone else. He keeps his hand raised, determined to leave it there until he gets picked. Mrs. Erickson told his mommy during a parent/teacher conference that he needed to participate more. He only wants to make them happy.

Felix launches a grenade at the back of Frankie's head. Felix is a bully. Felix does not like Frankie. Frankie does not like Felix. Felix has a talking dog. His name is Beast. Beast only talks about the weather and enslaving humanity.

The grenade bounces off Frankie's head. The entire class hides underneath their desks. The grenade goes off. No fatalities. Gold stars for everybody.

A little girl with pigtails walks into the room. She hands Mrs. Erickson a note. Mrs. Erickson reads it. Her lip quivers. She looks at Frankie and says, "Frankie, your mother has been in an accident."

The entire class laughs. Mrs. Erickson points at him, hooting and slapping her thigh.

CHAPTER 9

Frankie plays with his mommy's hospital bed. He moves it up and down with the controller. If his mommy were not in a coma and did not have a piece of ceiling where her head should be, she would say the hospital bed ride was more fun than a rollercoaster.

Frankie does not remember being a boy detective. He does not remember working on The Case of the Missing Heart. He does not remember his house blowing up. All he remembers is finding out his mommy has been in an accident and getting out of school early because of it. Yay! Getting out of school early makes Frankie happy.

Bones remembers everything. She tries to refresh Frankie's memory, but she can't talk so it doesn't matter. Frustrated, she tries to choke herself. Failing, she becomes even more frustrated.

Where is Frankie's daddy? Doesn't he want to visit Mommy?

Frankie wishes he were here. He would make everything better, as long as he didn't send Frankie back to school. He would cover Mommy in magical kisses and she would awaken as good as new. Their subjects would come from far and wide to bring them gifts and tell their king and queen how happy they were that their queen wasn't going to sleep forever and forever. The king and queen would spend the next two months writing thank you notes, but it would be worth it for all their new electrical appliances.

The nurse tells Frankie that visiting hours are over. He

hides underneath her uniform. She recognizes the signs of memory loss through the gap in her legs. She kicks him in the face really hard.

CHAPTER 10

Frankie's memory is back. He is writing in his detective notebook: a message for himself in the future for the next time he forgets. The nurse has taught him that giving himself brain damage with a blunt object will cause his memories to come flooding back. He bleeds all over the Kentucky Fried Chicken counter. His daddy yells at him, "That is not sanitary!" It is his daddy's job to yell, "That is not sanitary!" He manages the Kentucky Fried Chicken franchise. He is the big boss, so he makes his assistant manager do all the work. He will not let her yell, "That is not sanitary!" It makes him feel better about himself as a person. The assistant manager is old. She will die soon. Frankie's daddy sometimes has sex with her in the walk-in freezer. She has taught him so many things.

Frankie asks his daddy why he didn't visit his mommy in the hospital.

"Hospital? A zebra just dropped off an invitation to her funeral."

His daddy smiles. His son's hysterics ease the tedium of his boring workday. He waits for a few boxes of chicken to roll into the serving area before reciting his favorite phrase: "Just kidding."

Frankie shares his daddy's love for "Just kidding." It cheers him up whenever it floats out of his daddy's mouth.

His daddy blows his nose into a container of potato wedges. "I haven't visited your mother because I hate her. She is a stupid, smelly, fat feminine hygiene napkin. I hope someone drops off an invitation to her funeral really soon.

I hope it doesn't end with 'P.S. Just Kidding!'"

Frankie wishes he had a peanut butter and jelly sandwich. "Am I the reason why Mommy is a stupid, smelly, fat feminine hygiene napkin?"

"Yes you are. You left the place a mess after you moved out of her belly." He stares at the container of potato wedges. "Unsanitary! I will kill you, potato wedges!" He throws the container at his son's head.

The pain makes Frankie grow a little. Frankie's daddy doesn't notice that his son has grown an inch. If he did, he would say, "I threw the unsanitary potato wedges at your head to make a man out of you."

Frankie is glad his daddy doesn't say this. He thinks that potato wedges are delicious, but that the word "wedges" is icky when spoken aloud. It makes him think of the time he ate plastic octopus vomit. He is glad he doesn't have to think mean thoughts about delicious potato wedges.

Frankie's friend, Mr. Sun, shines his rays through the franchise's front window. Frankie waves hello. Mr. Sun does not wave back. Frankie is okay with this. He doesn't think his friend has hands. But Frankie is lucky that he doesn't know the shocking truth: Mr. Sun has hands and would feign nausea if he heard that Frankie considered him a friend.

Frankie feels frustrated. It has been a few chapters since he found a clue. This is what he does whenever his investigation hits a dead end: he removes his magnifying glass, aims it at Mr. Sun, captures one of Mr. Sun's rays, aims the ray toward his brain, waits for it to sizzle.

He perfected this technique on ants. It always enhances his deductive reasoning.

"I'm going to Grover's Cave!" he says. He says this every time he burns a hole through his brain. Grover's Cave is inhabited by a colony of clues.

CHAPTER 11

Bones murders a mysterious footprint. It was just a baby. This makes Frankie sad, but he won't give up his furry sidekick to the authorities.

They walk further into the cave. Frankie turns on his flashlight. It tells him that it was trying to sleep. Frankie imitates the sound of an alarm clock. The flashlight rubs the sleep out of its eyes and drinks its morning coffee. Frankie shines it on the cave's wall. Someone has pasted letters onto it. The letters were taken from the covers of various storybooks. They spell: A Savior Kitten, Yum.

Frankie scratches his head.

Can this be a secret message?!

Frankie scratches his head some more. It bleeds a lot. This only happens when he gets stumped or catches head lice.

Hey, kids at home! Frankie needs your help! Can you solve the secret message before he bores into his skull?

CHAPTER 12

Frankie listens to a bloodstained pine cone and a set of tire tracks. They are crying.

Frankie watches the bloodstained pine cone and the set of tire tracks. They are hugging each other.

Frankie smells the bloodstained pine cone and the set of tire tracks. They smell like a bloodstained pine cone and a set of tire tracks. They also smell like the poop of a freshly murdered mysterious footprint baby.

Frankie is sorry for their loss. He jabs his thumb into his temporal lobe. He does his taxes. There are no W-2 forms nearby. Frankie has disturbed the portion of his brain that causes involuntary adult behavior.

Look what you've made Frankie do, reader! Have you figured out the secret message yet? Need a hint?

It's an anagram.

CHAPTER 13

The comma flies off the secret message. Frankie solves it. He is very disappointed in you. You do not get to join his Junior Detective Army. Only smart kids get to join his Junior Detective Army. No stoopids allowed!

Frankie explains the secret message to you. He makes you feel bad. "When you rearrange the letters of A Savior Kitten Yum, it spells Take Your Vitamins. Whoever stole my parents' heart must work at the GNC in the mall."

Frankie realizes he is talking to himself. He realizes this is the first sign of mental illness.

CHAPTER 14

Frankie hijacks a car. "That is not a gun," the driver says, "that is a dog."

Frankie tells her that Bones is a deadly weapon.

She thinks it's adorable how he's jamming Bones' snout into her temple as if it were the barrel of a gun.

She drives him to the mall.

CHAPTER 15

Frankie does not like the mall. There are too many floors. He looks down onto the food court from the top floor. The devourers of international cuisine look like ants. He experiences dread. What if someone pushes him over the railing? He turns his head to see if anyone is approaching him. It's all clear. He tries to figure out why the entrance to the mall is located on the top floor. Did a colony of giant moles dig an enormous hole so people could have a place to buy pants?

An old woman walks by, carrying shopping bags. Frankie gets nervous. He vomits. The vomit falls on a family of giant ants. It ruins their Chinese panda lunch.

Frankie runs away. An imaginary mall security guard chases him. He gets away by telling himself that the big, brawny man isn't real.

CHAPTER 16

The GNC store is scary. It is filled with men who look like they're wearing tires underneath their workout suits. They remind Frankie of the monsters that he has seen in movies. He wonders if they will knock him over and trample him like a city. He wishes he had 3D glasses and a bag of popcorn. He removes a remote control plane from his junior detective kit. It flies around the customers' heads. It is very aggressive. The men don't notice, but it makes Frankie feel a little better.

He approaches the store's cashier. The cashier is wearing a black mask with a white question mark. Frankie decides to go undercover as a boy who takes his vitamins every morning. He asks, "What vitamins taste best?" He waits for a response. It takes a long time, so Frankie consults his detective handbook to find out how he can trick a confession out of his suspect with a conversation that begins with "What vitamins taste best?" He chides himself for not knowing: "Stupid! Stupid! Stupid!"

A skinny shopper runs into the store, covered in blood. "They're killing everybody!" he screams.

CHAPTER 17

Oh, Bones! Not another shopping mall massacre!

Frankie runs out of the store to calm his furry sidekick. Bullets whizz past his head. They debate whether or not it would be cruel to penetrate the flesh of a child. They decide to keep it PG-13 and head toward the nearest housewife.

Frankie puts on the bulletproof vest that Bones bought him for Christmas. Bullets hit him in the chest. It hurts a lot, but he is glad to finally know it works. He notices Bones peeing outside the Hot Topic while her paws work a machine gun. "Stop shooting me, Bones!" he says.

Bones loses interest in testing out her gift. She barks at a gang of security guards. They have guns. Frankie closes his eyes, hoping the security guards are imaginary. The security guards and his dog trade gunfire. They are not imaginary.

Frankie jumps into the crossfire. The pain makes him cry. The security guards point at Frankie and snicker. They lose interest in trying to neutralize Bones and aim for the stupidest kid in the mall. Their marksmanship improves considerably.

Frankie ducks for cover. He throws himself in a garbage can. The security guards take pity on him and stop shooting. There is nothing sadder than a boy detective who has to impersonate a piece of garbage in order to stop crying.

The security guards turn their guns back on Bones.

Bones shoots half of them in the face.

The security guards who won't have closed casket funerals during the next few days walkie-talkie for reinforcements.

The combined military forces in Afghanistan board a giant super secret plane that travels at the speed of instant coffee. The plane takes off. It flies across the Atlantic Ocean. It crash lands in the Bayport Mall. The soldiers escape from the burning wreckage one by one. They have more guns than Bones. She is really scared now!

CHAPTER 18

Bones puts down her machine gun. She runs away. The military does not catch her. They do not know where she went. They have not been trained in dog catching. They are a disappointment to America. They fly back to Afghanistan.

Frankie crawls out of the garbage. He removes Auntie Anne's pretzel crumbs from his hair. He goes back to GNC.

CHAPTER 19

The masked cashier has already gone home for the day. The store's manager tells this to Frankie while flexing. His biceps look like cans of tuna fish. They *are* cans of tuna fish. He doesn't want his customers to know he's a skinny wimp. How could a skinny wimp manage a store that sells performance enhancing "vitamins?" Unfortunately, he left his fake rock-hard muscles at home today, so he had to improvise. Frankie is the only one in the store who notices there is something fishy going on. He keeps quiet because he doesn't want to hurt the manager's feelings.

Frankie bends down to put on his "Long Lost Son" disguise. He says, "I am the masked cashier's long lost son. I would like be reunited with my daddy. Give me his address and I will tell him that you are a good person."

The manager hands him a free sample package. It contains a week's supply of chewable vitamins. They are shaped like mutants from a dystopian future. They are supposed to give kids the ability to beat up their dads. The manager has written an address on the back of the free sample package: 123456789 Street Road.

Frankie says, "You are a good person." He goes to the pet store to find Bones in her favorite hiding place. He shoplifts her. As he is leaving the store, a pet store worker approaches him. This makes him nervous.

"Detective boy," the worker says, "someone has stolen one of our dogs. Can you use your detective skills to get her back?"

Bones barks from underneath Frankie's pants. He shushes her. He agrees to take the case. The worker is pleased. Frankie feels guilty.

CHAPTER 20

Street Road is underwater. Frankie goes scuba diving. Bones holds her breath for a very long time.

They find the masked cashier's house. Frankie knocks on the door. It doesn't make a sound. No one answers because of this. Frankie rings the doorbell. It makes a foghorn sound. Frankie wishes he had a doorbell that made a foghorn sound. He remembers he no longer has a front door. He remembers he no longer has a house. This makes him very sad.

The masked cashier opens the door. He is now wearing a squid instead of a mask. The squid has a question mark stapled to it. Frankie thinks the squid is eating the cashier's face. He tries to yank it off. He yells for help. He does not have the strength to reveal the man's true identity. He does not have the ability to communicate with the emergency rescue fish that patrol Street Road.

"Stop pulling on my squid," says the squid-faced cashier. "I need him so I can qualify for tax-free status as a submarine."

Frankie lets go of the squid. The squid thanks him by stroking his face with its tentacles. "I am your long lost son," Frankie says, "and the manager at your work is a very good person."

"I've never slept with a woman in my life. Are you my immaculate conception? You must be my immaculate conception. I've always wanted to have an immaculate conception. Welcome to the family. Come inside. Let me give you a tour. It will all be yours after my death. Please don't kill me. I want to live forever. But forever seems like such a long time. I've changed my mind. I just want to live for a very long time. Please don't kill me for a very long time. Thanks for agreeing to suffocate me with a plastic bag after old age causes people to point and laugh at my formerly solid gold dancing abilities. This is the room where I keep my collection of regrets. One day it will all be yours."

CHAPTER 21

The room is filled with still-beating hearts. They are having a ping pong tournament. It is the semi-finals. The score is thirty-love. A heart with clogged arteries is winning.

Frankie throws off his long lost son disguise and says, "Ah ha!"

The squid-faced cashier looks down at Frankie's jumbo-sized baby bonnet. He frowns. He weeps. He holds his breath. He turns magenta. He has a hissy fit. He embarrasses himself. He scares Bones so badly that she hides underneath the ping pong table and whimpers. He puts a plastic bag over his head. He tries to suffocate himself. He does not have the willpower. He pokes air holes. He is the worst suicide attempter who has ever lived on Street Road.

CHAPTER 22

"Let's see who you really are!" says Frankie.

"Please don't compromise my tax-free status," the cashier pleads.

Frankie is overcome by the supernatural strength that is reserved for boy detectives whenever they're unsquiding their culprit and the squid is just a little too attached to its host body.

Frankie uses his deductive reasoning to guess the cashier's identity.

Hey, kids at home! Who do you think stole his parents' heart?

Was it Mr. DeMarko (now in zombie form)? A bad man with a very large brain? Felix the bully? Did Mommy do an inside job? How about Mommy's new chair, Bill? What about Daddy? His assistant manager? Frankie's evil clone? Old Man McNugget? Frankie's teacher, Mrs. Erickson? The Custodial Engineer Ghost?

Can't decide? You'll have to wait until the next exciting chapter to find out!

CHAPTER 23

It's Jesus Christ.

CHAPTER 24

Frankie is not surprised. All the clues have pointed to this conclusion. Jesus was his prime suspect this whole time. This confirmation makes Frankie feel a little better about himself. He is as brilliant as he has always thought, as sad as he has always felt.

"Why did you do it, Jesus?" he asks.

"Why did I do what?" Jesus says.

"Steal my parents' heart."

"Because my father has a crush on all of his children except me. I am getting revenge on them by love-heisting their homes."

Frankie Chinese-finger-cuffs Jesus. He calls the police with a silent, psychic scream. He can't wait to see his parents holding hands again. "Can I have my parents' heart back?"

"How am I supposed to know which one it is? There are many and they all look the same."

Bones licks Jesus' face.

CHAPTER 25

Frankie's mommy wakes up from her coma. Frankie is very happy about this, until his parents cut him in two. He does better detective work after the separation. The pain has made him stronger. He can dust for fingerprints in two places at once. He can solve The Mystery of the Exploding Home while being chained underneath the ocean. He can cry twice as many tears.

INTERLUDE

I call Frankie Nougat on my collectable *Sports Illustrated* football phone.

"Frankie Nougat Detective Agency," he answers.

"Hello, this is Bradley Sands. How is the case going?"

"It was really mean of you to get Jesus to steal my parents' heart and have them cut my fictional counterpart into two."

"My readers demanded it, so stop whining and tell me about your progress on the case. Have you discovered my novel's theme yet?"

"I've only investigated one novella, Mr. Sands. That isn't enough. I won't be able to detect your book's theme until I've gone through the rest of its novellas. I have found lots of clues so far, but I have no idea what any of them mean."

"That's a bunch of crap, Frankie. Don't you have leads so far?"

"Well, the theme of 'Frankie Nougat and the Case of the Missing Heart' might be about how children whose parents are getting a divorce often believe it's their fault, but it's not so they should stop feeling sad."

"Wow, Frankie, you might be the worst detective ever. The novella is about how your parents are about to get a divorce, you are responsible, and your punishment should be to get cut in two."

He starts crying. I shout, "Stop whimpering and track down my novel's theme or else I'll get your parents to *actually* cut you in two and that won't make you a better detective like it does in my novella, 'Frankie Nougat and the Case of the Missing Heart.' That was fantasy. This is reality. Getting cut in two won't improve your detective skills. It'll kill you!" I slam down the phone receiver and instantly regret it. Damn, I hope my anger didn't ruin the collectable value of my *Sports Illustrated* football phone. I get really nervous and check for damage. Nope, not a scratch. I feel relieved, but the nervousness remains. I don't understand why whenever the cause of my mental distress goes away, the emotional pain stays behind. I inject the contents of a bag of heroin into my right arm. My emotional pain goes away.

CHEESEQUAKE SMASH-UP

CHAPTER 1: THE DERBY

The Golden Arches were covered in blood and the Egg McMuffins were being sold at fifty percent off for a limited time only.

A Burger King smashed into its competitor, shattering its window to a chorus of cheers that were soon drowned out by screams. Fast food connoisseurs poured out of the McDonald's like vermin: crying, bleeding, clutching severed body parts to their chests. Some city denizens stopped to watch with ghoulish delight, while others knew when to get the hell out of the way.

The Home of the Big Mac levitated up and away from its attacker, heading toward the Walmart parking lot down the street. Reaching its destination, it stopped and revved its engine. Then it drove back to Burger King at full speed—plowing down the faithful customers who weren't able to pick themselves off the pavement after the first attack—and crashed through the front of the building.

Nearby, hundreds of buildings lifted off the ground and smashed into each other, turning downtown into a giant mosh pit. The skyscrapers and restaurants slam danced to the sound of their own destruction.

***

"Welcome to Cheesequake City, home of the fast food industry's first and last demolition derby. You're in for a special treat, folks. We've replaced the run-of-the-mill cars that you're used to seeing in this sort of competition with mobile buildings. And where else would you see such an incredible competition than in Cheesequake, the only city where buildings come equipped with levitating technologies.

"But this game isn't being played exclusively for your entertainment. Our government has decided to put a stop to the competition between all the fast food companies by forcing them to compete in a no-holds-barred battle royal. Winner takes all: a monopoly over the entire fast food industry.

"Each corporate headquarters will be competing in conjunction with the franchises that call Cheesequake City home. Some familiar names may be missing from the roster, and I'm saddened to tell you that those companies have been recently destroyed by the terrorist acts that the fast food barons have perpetrated against themselves. You can expect to see some eye-gouging action from the following companies:

Subway (with 301 franchises)
McDonald's (275 franchises)
Burger King (254 franchises)
Taco Bell (216 franchises)
Wendy's (201 franchises)
KFC (176 franchises)
Hardee's (144 franchises)
Arby's (112 franchises)
Carl's Jr. (99 franchises)
Popeyes (78 franchises)
White Castle (52 franchises)
Jack in the Box (42 franchises)
Whataburger (28 franchises)
Hot Dog City (12 hot dog stands)

NGA Corp (1 building)

"Wait! What are the NGA Corporation doing here? They don't own a chain of fast food restaurants! Umm…what is it that they do?"

CHAPTER 2: NGA BUILDING

The hot dog stand was just aching to be my bitch. I watched on my computer monitor as it sashayed from side-to-side. I wondered if he was trying to intimidate me? The giant wiener on his roof made a heck of a target, so I pointed my mouse toward it and slammed down on my spacebar.

Huh…this thing was moving really slowly. Even slower than an old man who was trying to cross the street in a broken wheelchair. The building crawled forward like a stagecoach pulled by hamsters.

I looked around the call center to make sure that no one was on to me. My co-workers had no idea that our building was competing in the demolition derby, and none of them ever would if the building managed to stay below the speed of a paraplegic. But hopefully I would be able to pick up the pace, or else I would need to come up with another super-awesome plan to win the derby. My current one where I harassed the little hot dog stands, ran away from all the other buildings that attacked me, and waited until they annihilated each other just wouldn't cut it.

No one seemed to notice that the building was in motion. Customer service reps were busy with their calls. Stuart, who worked to my left, was telling a caller to shut up so he could listen to rap music. Gordon was stationed over at the office supply closet, pulling out one of the few remaining hairs on his head as he chastised a co-worker for exceeding his daily amount of paperclips. Babs was busy adjusting her cleavage in the next cubicle over. Mr. Tomfoolery, our CEO, was going through rigor mortis in his office. The employees who worked on the other floors were at home, sleeping. They didn't have to go to work because their floors were under construction. I couldn't have picked a better day to get smashed-up.

Maybe the building's levitation technologies were malfunctioning? I looked out my window to get a better view. It was the only window in the room. The other employees despised me for having it. But since I'm a heck of a likable guy, they only held a grudge during the summertime since Mr. Tomfoolery was too cheap to pay for air conditioning.

I stared down at the street below. No, the levitation engine was working fine.

"I wonder if gramps will get across the street before I die of old age," I grumbled.

"Monty, stop harassing the elderly," Babs said, giving me an eyeful of her thong as she bent down to pick up a pen.

The old gal was sensitive about things like that because she was close to death herself. She was also very touchy-feely and I had to be constantly on guard so she wouldn't rub my funny spot. "My taste in men may have been extraordinarily picky during my first eighty years," she would say, trying to grab a handful of my boy-berries, "but now I'm making up for lost time."

Fifteen minutes had gone by and I still wasn't even close to running over the hot dog cart. Frustrated, I bashed my head on the desk, hitting my stapler on the way down. Then there was a ding, the NGA building picked up speed, and the cart made a little crunching noise as we drove over it.

Aaaaah! How do you stop this thing?

While my building fender-bendered everything in its path, I frantically searched for the brake, pushing every button on my keyboard—twice.

Someone tapped me on the shoulder.

I shot up out of my seat to block off the window.

"I'm embarrassed for you, Monty."

Oh, phooey! It was Gordon.

"Leaving your phone off the hook when you should be working, aye?" he said, recording my transgression in his notebook. "I'll make sure Mr. Tomfoolery finds out about this at my earliest convenience, which happens to be right now."

He turned, but the sound that a four wheeler makes after a building crashes into it at one ninety-eight miles an hour caused him to reconsider. "Whu…what was that?"

"The construction workers are getting rowdy."

"I'm writing up a report on those goons," he said, attacking his notebook with a Bic. "That kind of noise isn't appropriate for a work environment." He glanced at me as I tried to cover up the window with my body. "Did you know that you've stretched six times in the last five minutes, exceeding the company limit of five stretches a day?"

Gordon wasn't always such an anal-retentive prick. He used to be just a really boring guy who everybody hated to eat lunch with. But ever since the vice president of the water refilling department died, he's been brown-nosing the heck out of Mr. Tomfoolery, hoping to get chosen to fill the position. I had no faith in Gordon's methods. Mr. Tomfoolery was too smart to promote the office's new rat. The instant he made the announcement, Gordon would get a shiv in his back.

It made more sense to work really hard like the other employees.

But not Babs. She had a different strategy for promotion: seducing Mr. Tomfoolery with her prehistoric boobies.

As for Stuart, he was always reminding me that he didn't want the promotion, practically making daily announcements at the top of each hour that "vice presidents don't get to make whoopie around all day." Actually, he used another word; a dirty, dirty word that he can't force me to say.

But everybody except for Mr. Potty Mouth was in for a disappointment. The promotion was as good as mine.

I didn't think I had a chance, until I squeegeed my computer monitor a few days ago. I guess it hadn't been cleaned in like forever because removing the squeegee from its Velcro pouch made the building RRRRHUUUMMM like a monster truck. This was when I discovered that my computer was the building's control panel and my monitor squeegee was its ignition.

Soon after, I found out about today's demolition derby. Knowing that meat was Mr. Tomfoolery's favorite food, I entered us into the competition. After winning, the NGA Corporation would branch out of telecommunications and gain control over the entire fast food industry.

Mr. Tomfoolery would have no choice but to give me the promotion.

I cannot lose!

Well, I might have a hard time winning if the NGA building didn't stop accelerating until it fell into the ocean.

Wait…what the heck was I doing? How could I have possibly thought I could win? I don't even know where the brakes are located. I wish someone would teach me how to drive this gosh-darn thing.

I've had it! I'd swap my computer with Stuart's while he went on his next bathroom break. Let him deal with the derby while my life went back to normal.

I really needed this job. I had too many child support payments to make. I couldn't be fired for demolishing our office building. Stuart could take the blame. He lived with his mom. He didn't pay rent. He spent all of his paychecks on beer and novelty toys.

But…oh poop.

I forged the documents to register the NGA building for the derby. I accidentally smeared my fingerprints all over the entry form in chocolate. I wrote my own name in the signature line by mistake. I don't own a bottle of Wite-Out. I thought crossing out my name and writing Mr. Tomfoolery's in its place would be good enough.

I was totally whoopied. Mr. Tomfoolery was going to find out it was me for sure.

There's no way out.

I cannot lose.

CHAPTER 3: CRAPVIEW APARTMENTS

Scabies crane-kicked down the door, revealing an apartment filled with a thousand cans of hairspray that were stacked up to the ceiling. And with a swing of his black velvet cape, he lunged into the room, gun ready for anyone he might find inside.

"All clear, Bubbles," he said, his smile-shaped mustache glistening with perspiration. Then he took a bite out of a Big Mac.

Scabies' platonic lifemate pogoed into the room, moving with the intensity of a bouncy ball. He wore a fish bowl over his head. It was the only way he could exist in a world of humanity.

He was a giant goldfish.

A giant goldfish with severe pyromaniac tendencies. A giant goldfish who had just lit a butane lighter in a room full of flammable hair care products.

"Will you put that out?" Scabies asked, looking like he was about to shit his pants.

Bubbles stared into the flame and grinned with delight.

"Hey, you!" Scabies said, snapping his fingers next to his lifemate's ear. "Bubbles!"

The goldfish stopped pogoeing and grinning.

Frantic, Scabies removed his top hat and fanned out the flame.

"What's your problem?" Bubbles asked.

"You almost cremated us again," Scabies said, on the verge of hyperventilating. He was so sweaty that his wife beater looked like it was made out of Saran Wrap and it exposed a svelte figure.

Bubbles opened his eyes wide, as if seeing the room for the first time. "What's with all the fucking hairspray?"

Scabies looked like he was about to lose his patience. "I don't know what the cans of hairspray are all about," he said. He took French fries out of the sack that he wore around his shoulder and swallowed ten of them in one gulp. "I didn't know the first time you asked me that question and I haven't been able to figure it out during the last sixty-five times. I don't know why the majority of the rooms that we've broken into are filled with cans of hairspray instead of loving families. I didn't know we'd be hijacking a hairspray warehouse. The police aren't going to back off if we start shooting cans of Aquanet..."

Bubbles made an attempt to be helpful. "Well, maybe we'll get chased by the fashion police and they'll cater to our every whim until each can is returned unharmed."

"Cut the sarcasm. This is serious. How am I ever going to put McDonald's out of business when I'm working with nimrods like you?" he asked, and sipped a medium Coke.

Bubbles puffed out his cheeks. "I resent being called a nimrod."

Scabies looked at the fish's empty rocket belt and sneered. "And why in Steven Seagal's name are you wearing that thing? You don't even have a rocket launcher, let alone any rockets."

"It's a fish thing. You wouldn't understand."

"I should have just applied for a job at every McDonald's in the country instead of hiring you nimrods. I could have concealed rodents in their hamburgers and poured hot coffee on the crotches of old ladies when they'd least expect it. And when I was through with him, The Clown's legal bills would have been so astronomical that he would have had to file for bankruptcy and close all his restaurants. That's what I should have done instead of relying on others to take down The Clown. I hate McDonald's so much," he said, biting into an apple pie, "that I can taste it. I hope we have enough hostages. Maybe we can use mirrors and make the seven of them look like seventy."

"Don't worry, Scabies," Bubbles said, holding his lighter beneath a can of hairspray. He sprayed the can into the air and set the mist on fire. "Cans of hairspray are more flammable than hostages."

CHAPTER 4: NGA BUILDING

The NGA traveled over crowds of demolition derby enthusiasts, porcupine petting zoos, and city fountains that sprayed Tang. The building was out of control and there was nothing that I could do to stop it. Panicking, I tried various techniques: I slammed the side of the computer screen, sweated all over the keyboard, whimpered like a hungry puppy, kicked my desk, and prayed—but I still couldn't locate the brake.

Frustrated, I picked up my wastebasket and emptied its contents onto the floor.

Then the building stopped.

I was so happy I didn't even care that Gordon was standing beside me, writing me up for excessive perspiration, inappropriate outbursts of emotion, defying the separation of church and the workplace, abusing office property, and littering. I was absolutely thrilled about knowing how to stop this thing. Not even Gordon could take this moment away from me. Not even when he was marching toward Mr. Tomfoolery's office, impersonating an Imperial Stormtrooper.

I picked up the phone, waited for the light to blink, and said, "Thank you for calling the NGA Corporation. My name is Monty Cantsin. How may I help you today?"

"Hello," said a throaty whisper. "My six-year-old swallowed my dildo and the instructions said I should call this number."

I never knew what was going to happen after I said my greeting. I could end up talking to someone who praised my computer know-how after I asked them whether or not they had turned on their computer. An old crone like Babs could be on the other end of the line, telling me that "she's fallen and can't get up"—calls like that always stumped me. It could be someone who was a beginner tampon user and needed me to clear up her perplexity. Once a lonely old man called and told me that he was willing to pay ten ninety-nine a minute to find out what I was wearing, then demanded I take it off. And since Mr. Tomfoolery just threw me to the sharks without training me, I had no idea if fulfilling my callers' every desire was part of my job description.

For the ten years I've worked for the NGA Corporation, I've been winging it and making everything up as I went along. The calls must come from a variety of 800 numbers that rarely seem to repeat themselves. And I'm starting to think they might not have anything to do with NGA and get forwarded to my phone by mistake, but no one around here has ever given me a straight answer. "Is your six-year-old still breathing?" I asked.

A Subway franchise smacked into the front of the building.

Compared to the black monolith of the NGA building, the thing was tiny. So tiny that it caused me to rethink my super-awesome plan to win the derby: I would now attack the little guys who were one-tenth my size. At least it would give me something fun to do while I was bored silly on the phones.

I put a hole in the side of the Subway and the unfit mother on the phone said, "I don't know, but he has a giant erection. I think it's his first. I wish I had a camera..."

"Ok," I said, "what you're going to have to do is hang up, redial this number, and speak to someone who actually knows what to do in the event of choking. Can you do this for me?"

"I don't know," she said and forced a fake laugh. "But I sure can try."

While I waited for the woman to hang up her phone so I could take my next caller, the Subway franchise did a 180 degree turn and tried to destroy me with one of its remaining walls.

Stuart yelled, "Cool video game!" into my ear. "Can I play?"

Terrified he would discover my secret, I showered my casual business attire in a nervous sweat.

Gordon sprung into action. "Stuart, I'm writing you up for being out of your seat for more than fifteen seconds."

Stuart turned toward him and I sighed in relief.

"Gordon, I'm writing you up for writing people up without having the authority to do so."

"And I'm writing you up for not recognizing my right to make a citizen's write-up."

"And I'm writing you up for being a ginormous whoopietard," Stuart said at the exact second the Subway franchise caused our building to experience a 3.0 on the Richter scale.

Then Mr. Tomfoolery popped his head into my cubicle, and his rotting nose fell off and landed in my lap.

CHAPTER 5: CRAPVIEW APARTMENTS

The Syphilitic Kidz flickered on the TV and Scabies was not a happy hijacker. During the recruitment process, he placed special emphasis on the job seekers who listed "loyalty" as one of their special skills.

Loyalty was not watching cartoons instead of the road. Loyalty was not laughing at dumb jokes instead of destroying as many McDonald's franchises as possible.

Felix watched the television from the couch, oblivious to the string of saliva that was hanging from his eyeglasses. He was a talented driver, but Scabies hadn't hired him for his ability to drool in reverse.

Loyalty was not singing a lullaby instead of making sure the police didn't arrest them for competing in the demolition derby illegally.

Paulie the Sloth sat beside Felix, rocking a cradle containing an AK-47. His body looked as if it were shaped like a home entertainment center. But he was just your everyday overweight Mafioso. The arsenal of guns that covered every square inch beneath his suit was what made him resemble Super Saver Electronics' bestselling item. He liked to tell people they made him bulletproof.

Scabies and Bubbles had entered the apartment during the scene where the Syphilitic Kidz were trading their kidneys for video equipment. Scabies had been feeling calm as they entered the living room, but catching his driver goofing off had now made him a candidate for heart disease. He opened his mouth so wide that he could have swallowed a basketball.

Noise boomed through the wall, disturbing Felix's program. He banged back with his fist, yelling, "Can you be quiet in there? I can't hear the television over all the noise you're making."

Scabies gave him a wedgie, grabbed the TV remote, and turned the channel. The screen showed a Wendy's franchise plowing into their apartment building.

"Why are you watching cartoons when we're under attack?" Scabies asked, hands wrapped around Felix's neck.

Tired of waiting for a response, he let go and popped a Chicken McNugget into his mouth.

"My brain will explode if I don't turn on a television program once every few minutes," Felix said. "I thought I told you that during the job interview."

"You did tell me, and I called you a moron. Brains don't explode from not watching TV. It's a scientific impossibility. And I don't really care if some obscure medical journal documented your unique, make-believe affliction. If your brains explode, just keep driving. No more changing the channel. You grok me?" he asked, handing him back the remote.

Felix nodded. Then, anxious to control the building through the TV, he aimed the remote at the Wendy's on the screen and pressed a few buttons to strike.

Scabies gave him another wedgie. "Save your strength. I don't want you to attack anyone who isn't affiliated McDonald's. Lose the Wendy's and find them. Seek and destroy, my wage slave of calamity, seek and destroy."

Picking his underwear out of his anal crevice, Felix tried to outrun the Wendy's, but they kept coming, sticking to the side of the building like rubber cement.

Bubbles squinted his eyes at the franchise. "I know a way to get rid of that fuck," he said, pogoeing out into the hall.

A symphony of police sirens pierced their ears.

"Pull over and show me your license and registration!" megaphoned a cop from below.

"Paulie," Scabies said, "get your ass to the back of the building and make those cops bleed with your bullets."

"No prob," Paulie said, trying to pick himself off the couch, but the weight of his guns made this difficult.

After ten minutes of watching his man moan, sweat, and make a face as if he were trying to squeeze out a dry turd that was as big as his head, Scabies expressed his frustration by giving Paulie a headache.

Paulie bent over and guns poured onto the floor like he was a slot machine in a casino owned by a survivalist.

He managed to get on his feet and dragged them slowly across the room.

Scabies forced himself to wait patiently.

CHAPTER 6: MCDONALD'S

"Would you like to supersize your salad?" Jo-Jo asked, her eyes bursting with excitement.

"No," the customer said, trying to stare at her tits, but they were barely noticeable underneath her baggy uniform.

"I'm a vegetarian too. It's REALLY nice to have you here. We don't get many veggie lovers around these parts."

Jo-Jo wasn't against eating animals. She didn't let ethics dictate her dietary habits. But the taste of meat reminded her of earwax.

"Listen, you hippie," said the customer, "I'm no lettuce muncher. Why would a vegetarian even buy a salad at a McDonald's?"

"Well I do, because I get a discount," she said, trying to remain civil.

"I was just ordering a salad to be kooky and ironic. And I've changed my mind. I'd like you to slaughter a baby calf in front of me and use its blood for salad dressing."

There was an earsplitting crash.

"What was that?" asked the customer.

"Our building is competing in the demolition derby. I'm super excited about it!"

"You're full of shit."

"No, look outside," Jo-Jo said, pointing to the Burger King that was engaging them in combat.

The customer refused to look. "I didn't see anything going on when I came inside, you stupid bitch. Why don't you go fuck a piece of tofu?"

Jo-Jo jumped over the counter, yelled an "AYEEEE!" and dropkicked him in the face. The force of her rage sent him through the restaurant's front window.

The Burger King picked up the customer with a giant spatula and smashed him against Jo-Jo's building. It did it again. And again, not satisfied until his face resembled a Chicken Tender. Then it pummeled him to the ground.

Jo-Jo went out through the front door and gave the dying customer a look of disgust. "Tofu tastes like urinal cakes," she spat.

CHAPTER 7: NGA BUILDING

Mr. Tomfoolery opened his mouth, releasing a family of maggots. "What's this I hear about your phone being off the hook, Mr. Cantsin?"

"I don't know what you're talking about," I said, casually pressing the buttons on my keyboard in an attempt to get away from the Subway franchise that just didn't know when to quit.

"Mr. Liddy tells me you've been using this tactic all day to avoid calls."

"Gordon must have taken it off the hook so he could drive up the number of write-ups he's written today."

"Is this true, Mr. Liddy?"

Gordon scowled at me. "I would make Monty choke on his lie if it wasn't against company policy."

I wondered if Mr. Tomfoolery realized his decayed nose had rotted off his face and had been perched on my thigh for the past ten minutes. "Would you like your nose back?" I asked.

He snatched it out of my hands and reattached it with a thumbtack. A layer of skin peeled off his left cheek. "It's your word against Mr. Cantsin's, Gordon, but since I dislike his nasally voice, I will see that he's disciplined accordingly. Hmm, what shall I do to him?"

While he smirked with delight, trying to determine my fate, something fell out of his pocket. It looked like a crown that had been constructed out of yellow sticky notes.

"What is that?" I asked, pointing to the object.

"Something that is none of your concern," he said, picking it up. He staggered into the direction of his office, shouting "I'll think of your punishment later, Mr. Cantsin."

I had never seen him wobble so quickly. He didn't even bother to stretch out his arms in front of his body like he usually did.

The Subway launched another attack, creating a loud bang. Slamming his office door, Mr. Tomfoolery yelled, "Whoopieing construction!"

I decided to make a slight adjustment to my super-awesome plan to win the derby: I would now levitate away from little guys who were one-tenth my size if they happened to be better than me at driving.

Gordon pointed at me, gritted his teeth, ran a very intimidating pencil eraser across his neck as if it were a knife, and walked away, scrawling into his notebook furiously.

I went back to the derby, trying out my newest super-awesome plan. And the Subway never saw it coming. I swerved, turning the building quickly onto a side street, and the franchise crashed into the back of a truck that was hauling manure, causing an avalanche of stinkiness.

Stuart peeked back into my cubicle. "What video game are you playing again?"

I had to tell him something. "It's called Cheesequake Smash-Up."

"You know," he said, stopping mid-sentence to blow air into a whoopee cushion, "you probably shouldn't take your phone off the hook while you're playing. I'm sure you can do perfectly fine while you're talking on the phone."

He put his whoopee cushion on the top of his chair and sat on it, making it sound like he was on the toilet after winning a 7-layer burrito eating contest. My co-workers looked up, slightly less amused than I was.

He stood on top of his chair and shouted, "Excuse me."

Then he came back down and said, "Listen, guy, I know that you have a hard-on for Mr. Moribund's old job, but you'll never get the promotion if you keep getting in trouble. Not that I understand why you would even want it. Vice presidents have too much responsibility. I mean, you won't ever have enough time to play video games."

"I could really use the money," I said. "My entire paycheck goes to child support and I'm living in a bathroom stall at a gas station down the street."

Stuart's mouth opened wide in disbelief. "Child support? What the heck are you talking about? Didn't you tell me you were a virgin?"

"Oh, I am. But I used to bottle my sperm during high school and store my collection in the refrigerator. After I moved away, my mother sold every last drop to a black market sperm bank. And I didn't find out about it until I started getting letters from paternity lawyers. It turned out that there was an accident with my sperm. It had gotten mixed with the sperm bank's brand of vaginal lipstick and a gazillion women had gotten pregnant from it."

"Happens to the best of them, guy," Stuart said. "With a complexion like yours, you're just lucky you're not the last of the Cantsin family bloodline."

The light on my phone lit up. "I have to take this." I picked up the phone and rattled off a greeting.

"Yeah, hi," said a voice that was oozing in sadness. "Can you tell me if I'm supposed to cut down or across when I'm slitting my wrist? I always forget that."

Oh sugarballs. It was from the suicide hotline. How come I never get those callers anymore who ask me to tell them a joke?

Babs walked to her cubicle and sat down. Her suit was so skimpy that I wouldn't be surprised if it were from an era when fabric was a costly luxury. "Tomfoolery totally wants me," she said. "He just showed me around his office, and let me tell you, he's decorated it to look like he's about to have a Roman orgy. And it's not like the man's interested in anyone else besides me. He probably commissioned six dozen Real Dolls to bear my image. He'll be fondling all of my mannequin titties while I'm whoopieing and sucking him…"

"Hold on, you want me to whoopie and suck my wrist?" said the gloomy gus on the phone. "What does that have to do with my permanent solution to what my therapist tells me is a temporary problem?"

A Chihuahua in a sombrero lit up on my screen, glowing an alarming shade of red. Uh oh, Taco Bell wanted a piece of me and I still needed to finish the call.

"…and he poured a cup of water over his head and purred like a kitten," Babs said, whispering into my ear lasciviously while she licked my lobe.

A creepy-crawly feeling dripped down my spine and the Taco Bell pounced on me while I was busy being incredibly grossed out.

Trying to relive the joy of getting a joke line call, I asked my caller, "What do cats like to listen to after a hard day's work?"

The Taco Bell tried to drive through our lobby. They may have been unsuccessful, but the impact still shattered my nerves.

"I don't care what cats listen to! Tell me if I should cut up and down or side to side. Up and down or side to side!"

"Give up? Cats listen to meow-sic. Get it? It's like music, but it's a little different. It's meow-sic!" I burst into laughter. "Now doesn't that cheer you up? Haven't you lost interest in this silly up and down or side to side business?"

"Tomfoolery took off his shirt," Babs said. "His nipples sagged, weighed down by twenty-five pound barbells."

"That's it! I don't need to use a razor. I'm getting in my bathtub right now and using a microwave for a rubber ducky."

The Taco Bell continued its assault, getting closer and closer to turning the NGA building into pulp.

CHAPTER 8: CRAPVIEW APARTMENTS

"Why is there a bong on your head?" Scabies asked the gorilla as they stood in the room that had been designated for the hostages.

The simian ooked a response.

To avoid possible embarrassment, Scabies pretended to understand what she grunted. "Have the hostages given you any trouble?"

The gorilla nodded her head, charged at the group of hostages, and bellowed, unleashing a stench that could exterminate a colony of ants. The hostages cowered back.

Scabies pinched his nose. "Kill anyone that moves."

"HOOCK HOOCK HOOCK."

Scabies' cell phone rang.

"Hello, Scabies' crime scene cleanup service. This is Scabies...No, officer. I don't know how fast I was going...No, I'm not going to pull over. I don't have to pull over. I'm hauling a gaggle of hostages. And that means your commanding voice has no authority over me. I don't want to hurt anyone, but I'll start executing one hostage every twenty minutes if you and your cronies don't stop tailgating me."

One of the hostages sneezed. The man next to her moved to dodge her snot projectile.

The gorilla smashed both of their heads together, creating a pair of Siamese twins that shared the same gore-dripping head. Then she threw them out the window.

Their bodies crashed through the windshield of a police car.

Scabies turned toward the gorilla and growled.

"I'm so sooorry," he whined into the phone. "That wasn't supposed to happen this soon. If there's anything..."

He reconsidered his words. "Scratch everything I just said, pig. That was to show we're serious." Then, munching on a Bacon Double Cheeseburger, he hung up.

Scabies put on a mean face for the gorilla. "We need to have a talk about what should be considered 'moving' and 'not moving.' 'Moving' should be punished by death, while if they're 'not moving,' you shouldn't do a damned thing." He took a deep breath. "Sneezing and leaning back to avoid getting drenched in the mucus. NOT MOVING. Reaching for my gun and shooting me in the armpit. MOVING. Blinking. NOT MOVING. Fondling your hairy tatas. MOVING. Chest going up and down while breathing heavily. NOT MOVING. Trying to escape. MOVING. Grok it?"

Before the gorilla could respond, a fireball shot through the sky.

CHAPTER 9: MCDONALD'S

The morticians wore black hockey jerseys. As Jo-Jo watched them cart off her rude customer in a dump truck that was designed to resemble a hearse, she wondered if they played in the NHL and subsidized their incomes by working in the death industry during the off-season. She imagined a hockey game where a still-beating heart was used instead of a puck.

Her daydreams were interrupted when the Burger King franchise's giant spatula lunged toward her.

She slipped back inside to avoid capture,

El Jefe, her manager, had been waiting for her. "Why did you escort a paying customer off the premises?" he asked, sharpening his immense beard with a hedge clipper.

Jo-Jo tore out a few of her hairs as she tried to concoct an excuse that would get her off the hook. "Umm...he ordered an extra value meal, the number three, and demanded mustard on his burger instead of ketchup."

Satisfied, he let her pass. El Jefe ruled over the menu like a dictator and would not tolerate any alterations to its contents. Patting her on the back, he praised the actions that she took to defend his menu and asked if she wanted to drive the restaurant for a little while.

"Boy, do I ever!" she said. "Thanks so much for this wonderful opportunity, Mr. Jefe. I hope to make Ronald McDonald proud."

"James! Take over for Jo-Jo at the counter," he called.

James stumbled out of the kitchen, reading a copy of *The*

Conspiracy Times and smelling like a wet fart. "Hey, El Jefe, hey," he said, trying to get the big man to look at a newspaper article. Before his boss had a chance to refuse, he started to read, "Know WHY the beef supply is in DECLINE? Well, the INFORMATION that we're about to present to you is WELL KNOWN to THE MAINSTREAM MEDIA who have chosen to SUPPRESS it: SECRET Malaysian government UFOs have been roaming the countryside, MUTILATING cattle after FORCING them to compete in EXTREME tetherball competitions."

El Jefe flaunted his might. "Stop yelling arbitrary words or I'll toss you out on the street. There's a simple solution to the beef shortage," he said, licking his lips, "and all will be revealed in a delicious new menu item."

CHAPTER 10: NGA BUILDING

The brutality of the Taco Bell's attack shook the ceiling, sending a rain of plaster down on our heads.

Babs brushed it off like it was only dandruff and continued with her gross story, "He made me put on a tail and chased me around the room while he called for his mommy."

"Ok, I'm getting into the water now," said the sad sack on the phone. "I'm blaming you if the microwave cooks me a TV dinner instead of ending my pathetic life."

I realized that I couldn't do my job and win the derby at the same time. I would have to choose one over the other, so I chose the derby since getting a promotion was infinitely more important than helping people. This time, I would have to be more discreet. No more leaving the phone off the hook. From here on out, I would pretend that I was working, occasionally taking calls but being less than helpful. And I would have to do something about this Babs situation.

"I'm not even going to ask why there's a TV dinner in your microwave," I spoke into the phone, "but it should still be able to do the trick. Get to it."

"It's going to take me a while to work up the nerve."

"That's no problem, sir. I'm willing to wait until you see things through. But put the telephone receiver down while you're blubbering. It's not my job to listen to your drivel." I turned toward Babs and said, "Stop bothering me with your porny grandma fantasies so I can get some work done.

You've already killed one man and I don't want to be added to your kill count."

This was the official cause of death on Mr. Moribund's death certificate: "Flashed by geriatric while changing water bottle at cooler. Too terrified by fossilized breasts to notice water spilling on floor. Slipped in puddle. Fell down, losing his grip on bottle. Bottle landed in mouth, face-up. Drowned in ten gallons of Poland Springs."

Now that I had taken care of my distractions, I was free to triumph against the Taco Bell by levitating away as quickly as possible. But I still wouldn't know true freedom until I was in the clear—because man, I *really* needed to pee. That would have to wait until I got rid of this pigheaded franchise.

Ogar, the janitor, entered the room, carrying a broom. While he swept the plaster off the floor, he used his brute strength to try to get people to sign a petition to make him the vice president of the water refilling department.

I was about to use a school bus as a shield when Ogar punched me in the small of my back and grunted, "Sign. Petition. Now."

Fingering the keys to ensure a kindergarten class would be the ones who were facing extinction rather than my co-workers, I told him that I refused to sign his petition because I wanted the job for myself.

Angered, he gave me a bloody nose, knocked me out of my chair, and threatened to shove his broomstick inside my hiney.

Since his argument was very persuasive and I didn't think the petition would convince Mr. Tomfoolery, I gave him what he wanted. But I still signed it as Osama bin Laden to be on the safe side. And he went away to bother Stuart—who pledged his allegiance to the janitor's cause—leaving me to show the Taco Bell what happens when they mess with a desperate man.

After a few fancy maneuvers, I left them in a state of total bewilderment. Those taco scarfing ninnies probably thought I had escaped into the sewers.

I couldn't take it anymore. My bladder felt like it was going to explode. I got off my seat and power-walked to the bathroom, hoping no buildings would attack while I was away from my desk. But Mr. Tomfoolery stopped me on the way while I was crushing my peepee between my fingers in hopes that it wouldn't erupt without my consent. "Mr. Cantsin," he said, "get your butt in my office. I've thought of an appropriate punishment."

I tried to tell him that I was about to wet my pants, but he just stared at me with his scary, dangling eyes. The fear that they would escape from his sockets at night and look down at me with disapproval while I slept gave me no choice but to obey.

Mr. Tomfoolery's office was decorated to look like a Roman coliseum. Banners covered the walls, made up of pieces of copy machine paper that had been scotch-taped together. There was a throne at the top of his desk that someone had constructed with thousands of paper clips, wrapped around one another. A giant tank of water sat in the center of the room, shaped like a fighting arena.

My boss hid behind his desk for a moment and came back wearing a familiar looking crown of sticky notes and a toga that must have been a window curtain in a former life.

"Welcome, Mr. Cantsin. Welcome to the NGA Corporation's first annual Gladiator Games. Please take a seat beside me," he said, motioning to a pile of boxes.

I did as he asked, crossing my legs to get a little relief from my full-bladdered affliction.

"Try not to think of this as a punishment, but a feast for your senses." He blew into a trombone and said, "I, Tiberius Tomfoolery Caesar, proclaim that the games have begun."

I waited for something to happen. After a few minutes, he turned a shade of red, stared at the tank of water intently, and snarled, "Men, pick up your weapons and fight!"

I did not see any men, weapons, or fighting. I thought Mr. Tomfoolery might have been a little funny in the head. Maybe his brains were finally melting down his neck?

Mr. Tomfoolery began speaking very loudly as if he were a sports commentator on the radio. "And Falco Pilatesclass cuts off Titus Aquatis' head with his sword. Oh, what an upset! I thought Titus would last until the end. But, what's this? Euripides Pertinax has just hit Falco over the head with his morning star. Ouch! That's gotta smart."

Totally befuddled, I said, "Sir, is something actually happening or have your brains melted into soup?"

"When's the last time you had an eye exam? The gladiators are sea monkeys, you imbecile!"

I squinted my eyes and thought I saw little dots swimming in the water, but my urgent need to pee could have been playing tricks with my head.

"Did you see that, Mr. Cantsin? Cronus Caltavious just knocked Euripides unconscious with a bowling ball."

And before I was able to say, "No...I did not see that, Mr. Tomfoolery," he stood up from his throne, thrust out a fist, and gave the 'thumbs down' sign as if he were a scorned movie critic.

I don't know what happened next, but Mr. Tomfoolery announced Cronus as the winner, awarded the prize of allowing him to live for another day, and told me to get the heck out of his office and stop taking my phone off the hook.

I sprinted to the bathroom and slammed my body through a stall door. As I pulled my zinger out of my underwear, there was a loud crash and I found my feet slipping out from under me. Without any hands free to brace myself for the fall, I slammed face-first onto the hard, sticky floor.

Something had just smashed into the NGA building, and worse yet, I had also pissed my pants.

CHAPTER 11: CRAPVIEW APARTMENTS

Surrounded by cans of hairspray, Bubbles chanted, "Pretty flame! Pretty flame! Pretty flame!" trying to set the universe on fire. He pogoed next to an open window, spraying four cans simultaneously into a funnel that had a ring of fire around the end of it. A stream of flame poured out, heading for the Wendy's franchise.

But the attack was overkill. The restaurant was already a raging inferno. Employees and customers were fire-dancing in front of it, trying to remember how to stop, drop, and roll. Then the fish pointed his device toward a fleet of police cars who had driven next to the side of the building.

Scabies was so pissed off that he almost choked on his milkshake. Huffing and puffing, he blew the ring of fire out, letting the hairspray spring forth unmolested.

The stream of styling liquid sprayed into the police cars, giving them all stylish new hairdos. This forced the officers to pull over so they could admire their new looks in police-regulation hand mirrors.

Bubbles turned toward Scabies, looking as if he were about to cry.

"For the last time," Scabies said, stopping to relieve his frustration with a Quarter Pounder, "it's not safe to expose a room full of flammable chemicals to an open flame. The concept is pretty simple. You've already demonstrated it with that ridiculous weapon-" Then he vomited up twenty-five Happy Meals.

CHAPTER 12: MCDONALD'S

"I hate you, Jo-Jo," Harold said, sprinkling onions on top of a burger patty. "I hate your silly bangs and your dopey smile. I never had to deal with nitwits like you back when I was an aerospace engineer."

Jo-Jo smiled, lost in the excitement of battle. She was maneuvering the fry station's console, controlling the building with the tips of her fingers. "What's an arrowspace engineer?"

"It's pronounced aerospace engineer, you idiot. And I used to build rockets."

"Wow, you were a rocket scientist! That's so cool! When I was younger, I would shoot those little things up in the air. But I was never able to launch them into outer space. They always came down, and sometimes the parachute didn't work and they came down really hard."

Harold had lost his patience. He threw a Filet-O-Fish against the wall, almost hitting the retarded dishwasher, Big John, in the back of the head. The tartar sauce dripped down, making the wall look like it was the thigh of a teenager who had just woken up from a wet dream.

"I worked on real rockets, not that kid stuff. But the job market in that field is so competitive because NASA only launches one rocket every couple of years. And I should be driving this building, not you."

"I don't know…" Jo-Jo said, levitating the McDonald's down onto the Burger King in an attempt to crush it, "I'm preeetty good at it."

"You're delusional," Harold said. "That roof is made of reinforced steel. You're barely denting it."

Disappointed, she gave up and floated back to the ground.

Jo-Jo noticed a shiny red button. This excited her. She pressed the button and a cybernetic monkey's claw shot out the side of her building.

She aimed for her enemies' drive-thru window and pushed the button again, sending the claw through the window, where it snatched up the building's driver and gave him a horrifying ride toward Jo-Jo's McDonald's.

The Burger King spun out of control and crashed into the statue of a very constipated man on a horse, totaling the franchise beyond repair.

The monkey's claw popped into the McDonald's kitchen and dropped the Burger King driver into the top of an industrial-sized meat grinding machine. Jo-Jo was too busy stomping on the heads of the Burger King survivors to notice the screams.

Two dozen burger patties tumbled out of a panel, landed on the conveyer belt, passed through the oven, and rolled out in front of Harold.

But before he could put the first burger in a wrapper, El Jefe swiped it out of his hands, took a bite, and proclaimed its deliciousness.

He spat out a finger-sized bone.

Jo-Jo stared down at it. "Isn't that a health code violation?"

"The health code is my party whore," El Jefe said, "and bends to my every desire. She is as flexible as a sexy contortionist." He guided Jo-Jo's hand, causing the monkey's claw to once again visit the helpless franchise. "You like my secret weapon, yes? Make Ronald McDonald happy and attack anyone who comes out of that Burger King, kay?"

Jo-Jo nodded. Over the next few minutes, hundreds of bodies uttered their final screams while they were being carried toward her.

And the beef never stopped flying down from the ceiling. Frantically, Harold tried to trap as many patties as possible into buns while a never-ending supply of customers burst through the front door, demanding to sample the franchise's newest taste sensation.

El Jefe scrutinized the chaos and declared that the McDonner Burger was a success.

CHAPTER 13: NGA BUILDING

"Pow! Pow! Pow! Ratatatatat!"

Stuart was sitting behind my desk when I got back, pounding on my keyboard with his elbows. Three franchises were taking turns abusing our building. Stuart was even worse at driving than I was, and he didn't know he only had one life.

"Oh hey, guy. This is the best time I've had at work since mom gave me pot brownies with my lunch. Why do you smell like a urinal?"

I pushed him away from the keyboard and whispered in his ear, "It isn't me. Babs has a bladder control problem."

Stuart took an unhealthy interest in my window while I got us to safety. "Holy worm penis! You're moving this thing!"

"No, I'm not," I said, shoving my computer monitor in front of the window. This was the best chance I had to confuse him. I crossed my fingers, hoping that Stuart was the sort of guy who would mix up a window with a monitor.

He pushed the monitor out of the way and commandeered my keyboard. "We're in the burger derby, aren't we? I thought I was going to miss it because I had to work. This is the single greatest moment in my life," he said, crashing through a shopping mall.

I grabbed the keyboard back and drove out of the mall by way of JCPenney. "You can't tell anyone about it."

"Why would I want to tell anyone? It'll just end up getting back to the big kahuna and he'll send a company-wide memo banning fun in the office. I've always wanted to drive through a mall. I have an endless supply of things that I've always wanted to do that you can help me accomplish." He pointed to a spot on the screen. It was a CD store near the mall. "Let's destroy that place. They caught me shoplifting on my eighteenth birthday. Do it!" Then he crushed my fingers until we were headed in that direction.

Before I was able to get us back on track, we smashed through the store's front window display, decapitating a life-sized cardboard cut-out of R. Kelly.

"Wow, guy. That sure makes a lot of noise. How come none of the retards who work here have caught on yet?"

"The building's been under construction for a while, so nobody suspects a thing."

"That excuse won't work for long. Those noises are too intense to be construction worker-related. We'll have to do something else to cover it up. Hey, we should hire a marching band to walk up and down the halls playing Pomp and Circumstance. I *really* like that song."

"I can't afford a marching band."

"Oh right, that whole impregnating the entire universe thing. How about this idea? I can go down to the floor underneath us and bang on the ceiling with a hammer or something. I can cover up the sounds of extreme building battling with actual fake construction sounds. C'mon, tell me I'm absolutely brilliant."

I told him what he wanted to hear to get him out of my way. And before long, clanging noises were coming from downstairs. Problem was, no buildings were assaulting us.

I cursed Stuart's name, wishing him a lifetime of flatulence.

Then the corporate headquarters of Carl's Jr. attacked.

I couldn't believe that my favorite fast food restaurant was trying to kill me. I thought about their delicious Six

Dollar Burger with 100% Angus Beef and how they brought your food to your table instead of making you pick it up at the counter. I imagined the lips of that cute cashier who was nice to me that one time. I imagined those lips as they wrapped around my cheek.

For a brief moment, I was glad I lacked the skill to destroy them.

"You should flatten the doorman. I hate those guys."

Stuart stood behind me, waving a sledge hammer is if it were a flag.

"What the heck are you doing here? You should be downstairs making noise."

"I got bored."

"Well, can you go back there and make some more noise? I'm trying to get rid of an angry skyscraper here."

A huge hole exploded into the side of the wall, sending a handful of NGA employees toward their messy deaths.

They were all still talking on their phones as they fell, desperate to finish their calls before their shifts ended.

CHAPTER 14: CRAPVIEW APARTMENTS

Scabies' barf pitter-pattered into toilet bowl water. Bubbles was beside him, holding his hair out of the puke's way. The fish's rocket belt was finally serving a purpose: he could now carry cans of hairspray wherever he went. His homemade flamethrower was resting on the floor beside Scabies' top hat.

Stomach now empty, Scabies pulled his head out of the toilet and scarfed down a McRib. "I'm really uncomfortable with you seeing me this way," he told his fishy pal.

"Yeah, it's pretty fucking gross."

"I've never told this to anyone before, but I can't stop eating McDonald's."

"What a humongous fucking surprise," Bubbles said.

"No, I REALLY can't stop. I'm addicted to it. If I go a short time without it, then the withdrawal symptoms set in: headaches, sleeplessness, a stomach that feels like its home to a crocodile, heart palpitations, and beginning every word that I say with 'Mc.' Every time I try to quit, I'm in so much agony that I run to the nearest Mickey D's and kill my pain with an Extra Value Meal. The damn things are on every city block. The only way I'll ever make it through withdrawal is if McDonald's goes out of business and that's why I need to destroy their franchises and corporate headquarters. If I ever see that Clown, I'll gouge out his eyes so fast he'll be bleeding special sauce."

The Golden Arches whizzed past the window and Scabies nearly knocked the bathroom door off its hinges.

CHAPTER 15: NGA BUILDING

If I were to choose between having Stuart for a sidekick or a fussy parrot who sat around and ate crackers all day while he insulted my fashion sense, I would have to go with the bird because it would be less annoying. But Stuart wasn't totally useless. For instance, he was really good at covering up the huge hole in the wall with furniture. Now no one who looked at it will think we've been pulverized in an attack. Instead, they'd assume some crazy guy had been stacking furniture.

"Hey, guy," Stuart said, pushing the copy machine along the floor. "Can I drive for a little bit?"

"Keep your voice down. And of course not." I wasn't going to let Stuart goof off behind the wheel while we were still being chased by Carl's Jr. "Maybe later," I added.

Gordon blocked Stuart's path and said, "I'm writing you up for the misuse of office furniture."

Stuart kept pushing the copy machine, knocking Gordon off his feet. Even a nasty fall couldn't separate him from his notebook.

"How about now?" Stuart asked. "Can I do that thing that we talked about. You know, *that thing?*"

"Not right now!" I shouted, trying to get away from the Carl's Jr.

Mr. Tomfoolery came out of his office and glanced at the wall of furniture. "Why is there a hole in the wall?" he asked, clenching his jaw with such anger that his chin broke off and fell to the floor. "And why is Mr. Sutcliffe moving furniture in front of it?" He bent down to reattach his fallen appendage.

"The construction workers dynamited the wall to make room for your new, private swimming pool." Stuart said. "I'm covering it up because it was supposed to be a surprise. And now everything's ruined!"

Our boss put on a grumpy face, lurched back to his office, and slammed the door.

"Can I do it now? Can I can I can I?"

Worn down by Stuart's onslaughts and comfortable in the knowledge that the corporate headquarters had gotten tired of my gutlessness and gone off to fight someone else, I gave in.

"Don't worry, guy," Stuart said, abusing the buttons on my keyboard. "None of the other buildings will even know that I exist. I just want to drive around and frighten pigeons."

I tried to sit down, but I almost fell on my face. Stuart had used all the empty chairs to conceal the hole. So I leaned up against the wall.

I glanced at my computer monitor. It was filled with a crapload of little squares. Looking through the window, I saw hundreds of buildings in front of us, smacking into each other as if they were bumper cars.

This probably wasn't the best time to let Stuart drive.

CHAPTER 16: CRAPVIEW APARTMENTS

The Vain and the Vacant was on the TV when Scabies thundered through the door, screaming for Felix to destroy the McDonald's franchise. Within seconds, Felix found his tighty-whities pulled up over his head.

"If you blow this for me, Felix," Scabies said, channel surfing until his hated enemy filled the screen, "I'll split your head open like a pomegranate." He forced the remote back into his driver's hands.

The McDonald's had glided farther away from the apartment building since Scabies first caught sight of it, and Felix tried to catch up by increasing the speed.

The NGA building came out of nowhere and slammed into their apartment.

Scabies looked up at Felix's head, visualizing it as a pomegranate.

CHAPTER 17: NGA BUILDING

I wished I hadn't worn my teeny weeny purple polka dotted bikini briefs today. This was the thought that was racing through my mind as I fell to my death. Not "Golly, I wish I hadn't let Stuart drive!" or "Why was I standing next to the hole in the wall when I knew I was in danger of being knocked out of it?" No, I was worried that the demolition derby's official morticians would point at my dead body and laugh at my ill-conceived choice of underwear.

CHAPTER 18: MCDONALD'S

The manager now wore a giant, novelty cowboy hat for the purpose of shouting out the window. "Come down to El Jefe's McDonald's and try our newest sensation, the McDonner Burger," he hollered, as if the hundreds of crashing buildings outside were television viewers at home. "They're taste-tastic!" He shoveled one into his mouth and moaned.

Jo-Jo liked the word "taste-tastic" so much that she considered sampling the new product, but lost her appetite after putting a finger in her ear and smelling the wax.

Finished with his advertisement, El Jefe approached her as she steered the building away from a corporate headquarters. "That's right, my little chickadee. Defensive driving is the name of the game and your name is the young lady who preys on the weak, the half-destroyed, the easy pickings. You're gonna monkey-claw all the survivors and fill our customer's tummies with essential nutrients."

Jo-Jo did as he commanded, weaving in and out of buildings as they engaged each other in physical combat, scavenging the survivors. She was very good at her job, and the meat piled up to the ceiling.

"Woo-hee!" El Jefe howled, cradling a phone beneath his ear. "The corporate office is proud of you, my dear. And they're gonna back us up from here on out," he said, pointing to the enormous corporate skyscraper as it collided with an Arby's that had gotten a little too close to them. "They'll take care of any pesky critters who try to take us down."

"Don-ner Burger! Don-ner Burger!" The chant was coming from the front of the building.

Thousands of customers were crammed together in the room, human bricks in a wall of flesh. They continued chanting, pumping their fists in synchronicity as if they were at a Nazi rally.

El Jefe beamed at the crowd, exhilarated and trembling a little. "We need more meat," he said, grinning at the dishwasher. He grabbed Big John by the ear and led him over to one of the kitchen's microwaves. The retarded man clapped his hands, thinking they were playing a really fun game.

El Jefe shoved his victim's head into the microwave, smashed him with the door until he yelped, programmed the timer to cook his brains for five minutes, and pressed start.

The microwave turned on, giving off a high-pitched buzz. It wasn't equipped with the safety feature that prevented it from being used while its door was open.

Big John's head exploded, spraying gore over the faces of the kitchen crew. They stared at El Jefe, aghast, as he picked up the dishwasher's headless body and carried him over to the drive-thru window. Waiting until his monkey claw was nearby, he threw Big John into its warm embrace.

Man-meat rained down from the heavens.

And Jo-Jo finally realized what the McDonner Burger was made out of.

CHAPTER 19: CRAPVIEW APARTMENTS

A roof broke my fall and a mound of bird poop stopped me from breaking every bone in my body. I watched as the three hundred and thirteen floors of the NGA building drifted to the other side of the battlefield and pouted. Normally, the stench of evil that wafted off its pitch black paint job made me want to run home to my bathroom stall and hide beneath the covers. But this time, I only felt a desire to pole vault back to it so I could resume the demolition derby.

I was cleaning the bird droppings off my casual business attire when the building I was on top of lunged forward to avoid four White Castles, knocking me back into the poop headfirst. While accidentally swallowing a mouthful of the gross stuff, I realized this building was also competing in the derby. I wondered if its driver would be nice enough to drop me off at the NGA building. *Of course he would*, I thought as I went inside through a door on the roof.

I strolled down a hallway, trying to forget about the taste in my mouth by pretending to eat a hot fudge sundae. A series of grunts interrupted my dessert, and I looked up to see a gorilla lumbering toward me.

I did a double-take.

What the heck was a gorilla doing here? Was this building some sort of zoo? Would I find an elephant painting abstract art around the corner? And why were animals roaming the halls instead of goofing off inside cages?

Wow, the gorilla was really big. I mean, *really* big.

It stomped up to me, sniffed at my clothes, and looked disgusted.

I held out my hand. "Shake?" I asked, nervously.

It looked down at my palm and itched its back.

"Yes, Mr. Monkey. Let's shake hands and be friends."

The gorilla put out its paw, took my hand, and accepted my offer.

I couldn't believe how well-trained my new hairy friend was.

"WOOK WOOK WOOK," it said, continuing to shake my hand with vigor.

"Ok, you can stop now."

"WOOK WOOK WOOK."

It started to crush my fingers. "You really need to give me my hand back," I said.

The gorilla opened its mouth as if it were about to eat my face off and growled.

Before it could pop my pimples with his sharp teeth, I unleashed a high-pitched yodel.

The gorilla froze, clutching its ears.

I escaped through a door and slammed it shut.

What a weird room. It was filled with cans of hairspray. I wondered if the zookeeper styled his animals' hair each morning.

"Stoopid monkey doesn't know how to use a doorknob, huh?" I yelled, giving my hairdo a touch-up.

The horrifying creature charged into the door, leaving behind a gorilla-sized indentation.

I went out the window quicker than you can say, "Hello, police? Yes, I'd like to report an incident with a killer gorilla."

Now outside, I tried to enjoy the big battle, but I couldn't see very much from where I was hanging.

Gosh-darn it! It was a really crappy view.

The McDonald's corporate headquarters plowed into

the building. It nearly killed me, but I was able to grab onto another windowsill and pull myself away before it turned me into a casualty of war.

While the skyscraper mauled the side of the building, I swung to the other side where I was safe from its attack.

I was so exhausted from my workout that I collapsed on top of the windowsill.

I peeked through the broken window and saw a guy in glasses playing a video game. Neato! It was Cheesequake Smash-Up.

Oh wait...

"Felix, get the whoopee out of the way and let me realize my destiny," said a sinister man in a top hat whose voice resembled a wild hyena's. I wondered if he was an amateur magician because he wore a velvet cape. Or maybe he was the building's zookeeper?

Four Eyes handed him a remote control.

"McDonald's is going down like a midget on a tricycle who's just peddled into my lane of traffic," the top hat man said, working the buttons on the remote.

Then every building in the corporate headquarters' vicinity turned on it, launching a synchronized attack.

The gorilla scurried over to Mr. Tophat and started to play charades. I covered my mouth to stop myself from squealing.

It put its furry fingers together, creating the shape of a deformed face.

Tophat pushed the beast out of the way and kept fighting the McDonald's. The gorilla twitched its nose, smelling something.

Golly! The buildings were beating the ever living heck out of the McDonald's! It was almost on its last column.

The gorilla came over to the window and smelled some more.

The fast food buildings continued to work out their frustration on the McDonald's, with a Burger King and a White Castle sacrificing their lives to ensure its destruction.

The gorilla smashed its head through the window and glared at me with murderous rage.

CHAPTER 20: MCDONALD'S

"Honey, sweetheart, light of my life," El Jefe said. "Can you do me an itsy bitsy favor and turn the monkey claw on our faithful customers? We're almost out of meat."

Jo-Jo's job passed before her eyes. She didn't want all those people to die, but she really couldn't risk being fired. No one wanted to hire a fast food employee who had gotten herself canned. But she had already killed today. Could a few thousand more deaths be any worse?

Sensing her hesitation, El Jefe placed his hand over hers and forced her to bring the claw indoors, where it made fast work of the McDonald's customers, turning the front of the store into a ghost town.

He walked over to the cooking station. "Everybody must taste the new McDonner Burger," he said, plucking the burgers one by one out of Harold's hands before he had the chance to wrap them, "EVERYBODY!"

So zombified by all of the repetitive work, Harold hadn't looked up once to see what was happening.

El Jefe pushed a button that was hidden beneath the ketchup dispenser, and a portion of the wall lifted up to reveal a wall of cannons. Half of them were marked "naughty" and the others were marked "nice." He filled each of them with a McDonner Burger, lit their fuses, took a step back, and yelled, "Fire!"

The hamburgers soared through the sky, with the naughty burgers damaging buildings and killing people while the nice ones flew into the mouths of the hungry, who devoured them with zest.

"Hey, Jo-Jo," El Jefe said, "be sure and give those lucky, lucky people who are enjoying my burger the claw. It'll taste twice as good when it's made from the meat of someone who has experienced its yumminess."

Not being morally opposed to murdering customers and employees from *other* fast food establishments, she made all of his dreams come true.

CHAPTER 21: CRAPVIEW APARTMENTS

The gorilla was not happy with me. Its angry howl reverberated over the graveyard of demolished buildings that now surrounded the McDonald's corporate headquarters.

I leapt over to the next windowsill to avoid its wrath.

The zoo building bashed into the headquarters. The gorilla was the first one to feel the impact. Its legs had been severed from the rest of its body. I got off easy—the crash had only torn my shirt sleeve.

"That's what happens when you try to scare me," I said, watching the gorilla take its last breath as the corporate office collapsed under the strain of the attack.

Laughing manically, Mr. Tophat did a spastic happy dance to celebrate his victory. "The clown is dead!" he yelled. "The clown is dead!"

CHAPTER 22: MCDONALD'S

Dumbfounded, El Jefe gawked at the wreckage of the once great McDonald's Corporate Headquarters. Tears wiggled out of his eyes as he blew his nose into his beard. Then his sadness turned to rage. He jumped onto the counter, tore off his clothes, and proceeded to give what may have been the angriest tap dancing recital in the history of mankind, singing:

> *Attack!*
> *Attack!*
> *Attack that apartment building*
> *Attack!*
> *It eradicated our patron*
> *Winning my hatred*
> *And now, Jo-Jo, it must be destroyed*

Jo-Jo tried to hide her eyes from his naked body. It was covered in body hair. The hairs had been dyed green, making it look like he'd poured the contents of a Chia Pet seed packet all over his body.

Knowing she probably wouldn't have a job for much longer since the corporate headquarters no longer existed on this plane of reality, Jo-Jo climbed up on the control station, pulled down her pants, squatted, and urinated all over the French fries.

"*You* do it," she told her boss, wiping herself dry with her McDonald's visor.

CHAPTER 23: CRAPVIEW APARTMENTS

I watched the NGA building hover in the distance, its dark shadow passing over hundreds of wrecked buildings. No one followed. Except for a nearby McDonald's franchise, the battlefield was quiet, still.

The derby was nearing its end. Three competitors were all that remained.

I tried to get Stuart's attention by waving my arms, sticking out my tongue, showing him my tushie. But he was too far away to notice me.

I would have to take matters into my own hands and destroy the building from within. I would have to reach into my dark heart and kill everyone inside so there would be no one left to walk down to the winner's circle and I could claim victory for the NGA Corporation. This is how badly I wanted to be the vice president of the water refilling department. I was willing to engage in hand-to-hand combat for the first time in my life. And it was going to be a cinch. I've learned from the best: Kung Fu Stu on TV had shown me how easy it was to kill a guy.

Then the McDonald's franchise rammed into the zoo building, and I crawled back inside through the window for my own personal safety.

The room was full of people. They all sat on the floor and were staring at the walls.

Approaching them, I asked how they were enjoying their day at the zoo.

They didn't respond. Instead, they flinched away and

looked frightened.

I wondered if they were all mimes. Maybe today was Mime Day at the zoo and they had all gotten a discount on the admission cost? I threw a few quarters on the floor and requested the "Help! I'm Trapped in an Imaginary Box!" routine.

They just sat there and did nothing. If they were mimes, then they were the worst ones I had ever seen. Maybe they were beginners and hadn't learned the box routine yet?

"Are any of you competing in the demolition derby?"

They remained silent.

Since I had a soft spot for mimes, I decided to let them live. Bored out of my mind, I tried to leave through the door. Locked.

"Does anyone know where the key is?" I asked.

They didn't move an inch.

Unsatisfied with their performance, I bent down to get my change back and left through the window.

Choosing another one, I stumbled into a second room that was filled with hairspray and walked into the hall through an unlocked door.

Mr. Tophat was coming from the other direction. Flexing my hand into the Deadly Kung Fu Claw of Deadly Death, I waited to make the kill.

At least until I saw the monstrosity who was bouncing next to him: a giant goldfish, wearing a spooky fish bowl mask, carrying a funnel of fire.

I ran back into the room o' hairspray, muffling my EEK! with a closed door. After counting to one hundred Mississippi, I went back out into the hall to discover that it was now a giant goldfish-free zone.

I roamed the halls, listening for the sounds of my enemies.

I heard a BAM BAM BAM coming from inside a room.

So I went in, positive that it would be a good place to try out some Kung Fu moves.

A man in a suit was juggling four guns and pumping bullets out the window each time he caught a gun. The artillery didn't make any noise, so his vocal chords were providing the sound effects for them. He would have looked like Joe Pesci had the actor grown a couple of feet overnight and eaten a Winnebago.

I came up to him from behind and tried to chop his head in half like Kung Fu Stu would do with a stack of bricks. But my Kung Fu was weak. He remained in one piece and didn't even notice me. So I put my hands around his throat and squeezed.

He gasped, flopping his hands around. Bullets sprayed all over the room.

I tried to grab one of his weapons. He refused to part with it. Noticing his affection for it, I decided to give him what he wanted and let go.

He seized the gun with such force that he lost his grip and it fell out the window. "Oh my god!" he screamed. "My baby!" Then he jumped out after it.

CHAPTER 24: MCDONALD'S

Jo-Jo gave Harold a wet willy, hoping to knock him out of his work-induced stupor.

Color crept back into his cheeks and his lips curled into a look of disgust. He looked down to the burger that he was holding, perplexed. "Why does this beef patty smell like B.O.?"

"Oh, that's the new McDonner Burger," Jo-Jo said. "It's made from human flesh."

"It's made from *what?*"

James strolled into the kitchen, leaving a trail of blood as he carried his own severed arm. The bloody hand was clutching the newest copy of *The Conspiracy Times*. El Jefe was on the cover. Below his picture, it said, "CANNIBAL-ISTIC AGENT FOR THE SECRET MALAYSIAN GOV-ERNMENT?" James turned to the first page and began to read. "Know why El Jefe has TURNED his customers into CANNIBALS? Well, the INFORMATION that we're about to present to you is WELL KNOWN to THE MAIN-STREAM MEDIA who have chosen to SUPPRESS it: He's a SLEEPER agent for the SECRET Malaysian government. They've MIND CONTROLLED him into BELIEVING that he's a MCDONALD'S manager. Earlier today, a GREY ALIEN who has been working in CONJUNCTION with the Malaysians came into El Jefe's establishment to give him the PASSCODE PHRASE that ACTIVATED his mission. The word was "McGriddle."

A stream of flame shot through the wall, setting the

kitchen on fire.

Harold picked up a fire extinguisher. "I don't want to work here anymore if we're going to serve human flesh," he said, spraying the room with foam. "But I'm afraid to quit. Who's going to hire an aerospace engineer with a stint as a fast food cook on his resume?"

"We'll probably lose our jobs at the end of the derby anyways," said Jo-Jo. "Our corporate headquarters has been destroyed."

Harold choked on his spittle.

"But even if our building wins," she said, "I don't think I want to work for El Jefe anymore. I don't know what I'm going to do. I *really* need this job."

James read from his newspaper, looking light-headed and confused from all the blood loss. "Don't know what to do about El Jefe? Well, the INFORMATION that we're about to present to you is WELL KNOWN to THE MAINSTREAM MEDIA who have chosen to SUPPRESS it: Jo-Jo should murder El Jefe, cut off his SKIN, and take over his IDENTITY by WEARING it. Then she can BE our BOSS and the SURVIVORS from CORPORATE won't ever KNOW the DIFFERENCE."

Jo-Jo grabbed the newspaper out of his hands and looked at it. "James, you're hallucinating. It doesn't say that."

"I can hear you, you know!" El Jefe shouted from the fry station as he fought Crapview Apartments to a standstill.

CHAPTER 25: CRAPVIEW APARTMENTS

I kung fu hustled into the room to find Mr. Foureyes battling a McDonald's with a TV remote. Guns decorated the floor, and even though Kung Fu Stu always frowned while in the presence of firearms, I reached for one, gung ho about blowing my enemy's brains all over the television screen.

While I struggled to lift a gun off the floor, Mr. Foureyes interrupted me with a variety of questions and comments including "Who are heck you?" and "You're not supposed to be in here," and "Why do you smell like my suicidal hamster after he tries to drown himself in the toilet?"

I stopped trying to lift the gun, went to snatch the remote control from Mr. Foureyes, knocked it out of his hands, threw him off the couch, and put him in a figure four leg lock like the one Kung Fu Stu did during the episode where he joined a pro wrestling league to kill a bad guy.

Face twisted in a mask of pain, Mr. Foureyes reached for the TV remote, but it was too far away.

He started to shriek. "Must...watch TV...or brain will... explode."

I snickered at the silliest excuse that had ever been used to break out of a figure four leg lock.

Mr. Foureyes pounded on the floor with his fists, pleaded for mercy, and offered me his life savings.

His head popped like a frozen burrito in a thermonuclear chamber.

I loosened my wrestling hold, feeling really bad about not believing him. I looked over at his headless torso and started to freak out. It wasn't cool looking like in a horror movie. Instead, it was really upsetting. I couldn't understand why a dead thing was more terrifying than a monstrous gorilla who wanted to kill me. An image of the gorilla's death popped into my head, and I freaked out even more.

Hyperventilating, I pushed the couch on top of Mr. Foureyes' corpse to hide his hideousness.

After calming myself down, I decided to take control of the navigational system, so I plucked the remote control off the floor and aimed for the NGA building. The McDonald's franchise was still hot on my tail.

Mr. Tophat exploded through the door, yip-yapping, "Felix, why in Steven Seagal's name are you running away from McDonald's? We can destroy them without even breaking a sweat."

He noticed Mr. Foureye's corpse, looked at me, and glared.

I gave him my best poop-eating grin.

He called out into the hall, "Bubbles, sic this vermin."

The giant goldfish put down its funnel of fire and leapt into the room, looking ravenous for fish food.

I panicked and tried to crawl through the window. But before I could escape, it thrust itself toward me.

I went into defense mode—putting my hands over my eyes.

Something cold and hard hit my elbow, and I heard the sound of shattering glass. Opening my eyes, I saw the fish's bowl lying on the floor in a zillion pieces. And next to the broken bowl, the fish lay, doing the flippity-floppity dance.

After half a minute of solid gold dancing, the fish was still, his tongue hanging out of his mouth.

"You've killed my platonic lifemate," Mr. Tophat cried.

The last thing that I saw was the NGA building's front door and the tips of Mr. Tophat's pinkies as they poked me in the eyes.

CHAPTER 26: MCDONALD'S

El Jefe celebrated his triumph over Crapview Apartments by swallowing a bunch of McDonner Burgers whole like they were pills. Eyeballing the final resting place of the apartment building's ruins—a hole in the front of the NGA building—he dreamt of a McDonner Burger in every household. It would make all other foods obsolete, conquering the three meals of the day.

Desperate to keep her job, Jo-Jo interrupted his reveries with a "I won't quit if you stop with all the cannibal ickyness. Let's forget today ever happened."

"I have a better idea," El Jefe said. "From now on, the McDonner Burger will be the *only* item on our menu, and if you want to continue working for McDonald's, you'll have to do a few...umm...favors for me." He waved his penis around as if it were a conductor's baton. "Quid pro quo, Miss Jo-Jo, quid pro quo."

El Jefe gobbled down another burger, clutched his throat, and sputtered, "I...think...I'm...choking."

Jo-Jo watched her boss as he turned blue. She didn't know the Heimlich maneuver, but even if she had, she wouldn't have used it to save his life.

El Jefe let out his final belch.

CHAPTER 27: NGA BUILDING

I woke up with my arms wrapped around last night's sexual conquest. I lay in the warm, erotic glow, trying to reconstruct the events of our encounter. She must have headbutted me a whole lot of times because I didn't remember a thing. But maybe it was better this way. This was the first time that I ever dipped my zinger into a vavavoom. No doubt it had been an awkward, slimy experience. Now I could choose how I wanted to remember it. And let me tell you, I was absolutely sensational.

Trying not to wake up my honeypot, I nuzzled her arm as gently as possible and ended up getting her body hair stuck in my teeth. How peculiar.

I noticed she was still wearing a hat and that it happened to be a top hat. Curiouser and curiouser.

Then her crotch caught my eye. I contemplated her unsightly bulge and memories of the demolition derby and Mr. Tophat flooded into my head.

Now that I was fully awake and filled with disappointment, I looked around the room. It had been totally destroyed and Mr. Tophat was unconscious.

I heard the trickle of urine coming from outside. Through the window, I saw the fountain from the NGA building's lobby, topped with a statue of Mr. Tomfoolery's father as he passed a kidney stone. I crawled forward to get a closer look.

"Don't make another whoopieing move," a voice said.

I turned to give the speaker a piece of my mind about

his dirty mouth and screamed.

The giant goldfish was hopping up and down beside me.

"Aaaaah! Begone, zombie goldfish!"

"I was just pretending to be dead, you whoopieing moron," he said, then his teeth crunched down on my ear.

The pain shot straight through to my tear ducts. I whipped my head around, trying to knock the fish off my ear, but he didn't budge. I was surprised how light he was for such an enormous monster of the sea.

I jumped through the window to test the fish's tolerance for broken glass and landed in the fountain. The water must have made him stronger because he bit down even harder.

I gave the lobby the once-over. The zoo building was lying inside the room, totally destroyed. It had been smooshed together, reduced to one-hundredth of its size and now resembled a very large accordion. The thrill of victory rushed through my body, almost overpowering the agony in my ear. I only hoped the NGA building was still operational and the pesky McDonald's franchise hadn't won the derby.

I raced toward the elevator, longing to find out the status of things and to see if Stuart had any tips for getting the giant goldfish off my ear. Once inside, I pressed the button for the ninety-seventh floor, which was where I worked.

"Hold the elevator, please!" shouted Mr. Tophat. For some reason, maybe because of my ingrained politeness habit, I did as he asked. Once I realized what I was doing, I started banging my head on the wall and tapping intensely on the door-close button. But it was already too late. Huffing and puffing, he had made it inside the elevator.

A hairy paw grabbed him by the nape of his neck and pulled him back into the lobby. "Sign. Petition. Now."

I waved to Ogar the janitor as the elevator doors closed.

He elbowed Mr. Tophat in the face and a spurt of his victim's blood shot out through the crack in the door and dripped down my shirt.

As the elevator went up, I punched the fish, repeatedly, in the nose. His counterattack was to scratch my face with his fins, which was actually somewhat pleasant since it made me forget about the pain in my ear for a little while.

But it didn't last. The pain soon shot back, full blast.

Sick and tired of the torment, I tried to get the fish off of me by yanking as hard as I could.

It worked, but I suddenly found myself in tremendous agony.

I watched the fish as he flopped to the ground. Blood poured out the side of my head, showering him in red.

My ear was still in his mouth.

CHAPTER 28: MCDONALD'S

"I don't think I'll ever get used to this beard," Jo-Jo said, now wearing El Jefe's skin.

"You'll have to," Harold said, smoothing down a wrinkle in her new forehead. "El Jefe treated it like a head of lettuce that he was going to enter in the state fair. You'll never convince the board of trustees if you shave it. Not only will you lose your job, but you'll also buy yourself a murder charge. But do whatever you like. I don't care who's ordering me around as long as I don't have to cook McDonner Burgers."

Jo-Jo tied a scrunchie around her new beard. It made it look like the shape of a fist. "Do you think Corporate will suspect anything if I keep it like this?" she asked.

"You're pushing it," he said. "How does it feel under there by the way? All gooey?"

"It's like I'm swimming in a vat of liquefied gummy worms. I hate it. Not only do I feel totally nasty, but this thing is really creeping me out. I can't believe I'm actually going through with one of James' ideas. Next I'll be looking over my shoulder for agents of the SECRET Malaysian government. Well, back to the fry station," she said and returned to her post, eager to put the NGA Corporation out of business.

CHAPTER 29: NGA BUILDING

The elevator door opened as I threatened to bite off the goldfish's ear for payback.

Gordon was there to greet me. "I hope you enjoyed your extra-long lunch break, Monty. It'll be the last one you'll ever take after I report it to Mr. Tomfoolery. What's that smell? All employees must wash themselves properly before visiting the office. And what's this? You've dared to enter the office without an ear? Company policy mandates that all employees must be in possession of both ears while on the call center floor. And now you're littering again? All droplets of blood must be disposed of in a proper trash receptacle instead of on the floor. Failure to do so—"

He was interrupted when a mechanical claw wrapped its fingers around his body and pulled him out of the building through the hole in the wall. He remained calm as he flew through the air and began to write in his notebook. He was probably writing up the claw for interfering with his work.

I rushed to my cubicle, followed by the goldfish. He was moving very slowly, wheezing like an asthmatic.

Stuart was sitting in my chair, pressing buttons with his tongue. He saw me and took a breather. "Hey there, guy. Cool wound! Guess what? I've discovered that my tongue is a much better driver than I am."

I motioned over to my pursuer. "Do you have any suggestions for dealing with that fish? I think he wants to tear off all my body parts."

"You should buy him a fake, decorative castle to play in. It would make him a very happy fish and he'll forget all about his sadomasochistic tendencies."

My monitor flashed red to indicate danger. The McDonald's franchise was climbing up the side of our building with its claw and shooting burgers at the walls.

Stuart tried to shake them off with his tongue.

Mr. Tomfoolery staggered by, glanced at Stuart, and stopped dead in his tracks. "Why are you tasting the keyboard, Mr. Sutcliffe?" he said, getting angrier with each breath. "And where is Mr. Liddy? Why is there blood all over the floor?" His face was flushed red and he was shaking. "What is climbing up the side of my building?" His skin had turned the color of burnt toast and sizzled like a frying pan. "Why does the call center look like it's been hit by a comet?" He turned toward me. "Why…"

Then a burger smashed through the window and landed in his mouth.

Mr. Tomfoolery bit down, with hesitancy.

Satisfied, he hungrily devoured it, teeth grinding like a buzz saw. "That was the most scrumptious meal I've *ever* tasted," he said, plopping himself down onto the floor to have a food-induced orgasm.

I smelled the stink of fish. He had finally caught up with me.

"I'm gonna chew out your whoopieing intestines," the goldfish hissed menacingly.

I squealed and ran away.

I watched as the fish flopped toward me from across the room. I felt relieved. At the speed he was traveling, it would take him a week to catch up with me.

But then he hijacked the office's mail cart by threatening to commit a federal offense: opening mail that didn't belong to him. Taking the fish's threat very seriously, the mailroom guy did as he was told and gave the fish a big push into my direction.

Anxious to get out of the cart's way, I ducked into Mr. Tomfoolery's office.

I heard a crash.

The goldfish came into the office, riding the mail cart like a skateboard.

He hopped out of the cart and lunged toward my healthy ear.

I dodged his attack and he belly-flopped into the gladiator tank.

The fish let out an underwater shriek as tiny puncture marks appeared on his face, and the water filled with his blood. Within seconds, the sea monkeys had stripped him of flesh and his skeleton floated to the surface.

Overjoyed about his death, I went back to my seat. Stuart was giving his armpits a chance to drive.

"What the heck are you doing? That McDonald's is about to crush us into a pancake!"

I reached for the keyboard, and stopped when the elevator door opened and Mr. Tophat strolled out of it, covered in bruises. Our eyes met.

He charged.

The door to the staircase crashed open and oodles of police officers with stylish hairdos swarmed onto the floor. "Stop where you are, Scabies Awful-Awful, or we'll brutalize the criminality out of you."

Babs blocked the officers' path. "Hey, cuties," she said. "How would you like to satisfy all of my erotic needs?"

The cops took off their pants and lined up in front of her. The first man on the scene said, "Ma'am, let's make this quick. We have urgent police business to attend to."

She complied and the officer inspected her antique vavavoom with his fleshstick.

I felt cold metal on my chin.

"Tell me where Bubbles is or I'll make you bleed with my bullets," Mr. Tophat said.

I shrugged. "Who's Bubbles?"

He poked me harder with his gun. "My platonic lifemate. He's a giant goldfish."

"*Oh*," I said. "Sorry, but he was just killed by a bunch of sea monkeys."

"No, *really*, where is he?"

I pointed to Mr. Tomfoolery's office.

He walked away.

After hearing Babs slurp and moan for the next few minutes, Mr. Tophat came out of the office, carrying the goldfish's skeleton. Weeping, he lifted his former platonic lifemate up into the air and shouted, "No!"

Taking advantage of his grief, I knocked the gun out of his pants.

The weapon slid across the room and left the building through the hole in the wall.

Mr. Tophat crouched into fighting stance and punched me in the arm. His attack was accompanied by a "boomshakalaka" battle cry.

Shrugging off the pain, I grabbed a handful of his velvet cape and swung him around the room, smashing his body into a variety of office furniture. But before I could dish out the appropriate amount of revenge for making my arm hurt really bad, the cape ripped and we both toppled to the ground.

Mr. Tophat's hat slipped off his head as he fell down, revealing a set of pigtails.

I crawled over and put him in a bear hug. We tumbled around the room, screaming, biting, and pulling each other's hair. He scratched my chest, leaving marks, raw and sore. I tried to give him a taste of his own wussyness, but my attack was useless because I had clipped my nails last night.

"I could really use a Big Mac right now," he said, sweating like a tourist on a tropical island, and he puked all over my shoes. Then he tried to disfigure me with a stapler.

I tried to get him to stop by stabbing him with a handful of thumbtacks.

But he didn't seem to notice. He kept pounding the staples into my flesh and grinning maniacally.

Fed up and on the verge of passing out from the agony, I unleashed my secret weapon—my spot-on impression of a shark—and nibbled on the lower half of his body.

He yelped. "Did you just bite my dick?"

I swished the saliva around my mouth, tasting its flavor. "Yeah, I think so," I said, shocked by my behavior and ashamed of myself.

Enraged and foaming at the mouth, Mr. Tophat tried to knock my teeth out.

The mechanical claw hovered nearby as he pummeled my head. While he brought the pain, I struggled to direct the claw toward him like an air traffic controller, but it didn't follow my instructions.

"Stop hitting me!" I pleaded. He continued with his assault, so I kung fu kicked him with both of my feet. It knocked him toward the claw, which scooped him up and lifted him away as he wailed.

I noticed Stuart wasn't in my seat. The McDonald's franchise was still attached to the side of our building, and there was nobody behind the wheel.

I searched the room for Stuart, but he was nowhere in sight. Except for Babs and her male companions, the room was so empty that it was starting to feel like a Sunday. I wondered if the claw had escorted Stuart off the premises along with my other co-workers.

Then Stuart waved to me through the window. He was standing inside the McDonald's franchise, ordering food.

Flabbergasted by his betrayal, I hurried to my cubicle and grabbed the controls. The McDonald's might have been aggressive, but I had the advantage of being a hundred times bigger than it. All it took to end Ronald McDonald's reign of terror over the digestive systems of the American people was one little maneuver: I tilted the side of the NGA building toward the ground and brought it crashing down on top of the franchise.

CHAPTER 30: MCDONALD'S

Jo-Jo leaned against the counter. It was the only thing stopping her from being hurled into the call center below. The McDonald's was now pointing down as if it were a slide and its entrance had been replaced by a row of cubicles.

Stuart stood on the other side, propping himself up on the condiments rack as he ate from a container of fries. His clothes were ripped and blood dripped from his nose, bathing the fries in his plasma. This didn't seem to bother him as he crammed twenty bloody French fries into his mouth.

"Why is there a McDonald's in the building?" Mr. Tomfoolery asked from down below, looking as if he were about to go on a killing spree.

Stuart dipped a fry in barbecue sauce. "This is our new snack bar. And all of us at the NGA Corporation just want to thank you for the tasty grub."

Mr. Tomfoolery exploded in rage. "Do you think I'm stupid, you imbecile?"

Stuart nodded his head, caught himself, and switched to shaking it.

"This isn't a snack bar. I didn't order the construction of a snack bar. Why has a goddamn McDonald's crashed into the side of my building?" His eyes widened in understanding. "Who's responsible for using my building to compete in today's demolition derby?"

CHAPTER 31: NGA BUILDING

"I am," I shouted, feeling like the happiest call center employee in Cheesequake.

CHAPTER 32: MCDONALD'S

"I'm going to scoop out your brains and use your skull as a urinal in my private bathroom," Mr. Tomfoolery snarled.

He noticed a McDonner Burger by his foot, which caused him to release a gallon of drool. His pupils rolled to the back of his head.

"You there with the marvelous beard," he said, addressing Jo-Jo. "I would like to purchase this burger."

"I'm sorry, sir," she said, "but we're no longer selling that item. Can I interest you in a Big N' Tasty?"

"I'm prepared to offer you one million dollars for this hamburger," he said, taking out his checkbook.

Her eyes looked like they were about to leap out of her sockets. "In that case, you can have all the McDonner Burgers in the restaurant, but I still can't sell you that particular one. It would be a health code violation. There seems to be a man attached to it."

Mr. Tomfoolery noticed that the burger consisted of one half patty and one half Scabies. Again, he salivated.

"Our meat grinding machine must have malfunctioned when your building destroyed ours," she said.

"This looks like a perfectly good burger to me and I would love to sink my teeth into it. I can make the health code inspector a very wealthy man," he said, fanning himself with his checkbook.

Scabies let out a whimper and scurried between Mr. Tomfoolery's feet, escaping into the call center.

The CEO sighed and wrote Jo-Jo a check. "I don't have

the time to hunt for my own food. I am a very busy man."
He folded a check into a paper airplane, threw it at her head,
picked up the nearest McDonner Burger, and gobbled it
down.

A man in a plastic toupee scaled down the wall in suction
cup shoes and said, "Congratulations, Tom Tomfoolery, for
winning Cheesequake City's demolition derby. Donna, show
Mr. Tomfoolery the prize that he's won today."

A voluptuous blonde dropped through the ceiling in a
parachute and waved a board game from side to side.

"It's an iron-clad monopoly over the entire fast food
industry," the man said.

Reaching for seconds, Mr. Tomfoolery grinned so wide
that his lips rolled down his chin.

CHAPTER 33: DONNER BURGER

I stood inside the first Donner Burger franchise, filling up the drinks dispenser with water. This was my first official act as the vice president of the NGA Corporation's water refilling department and boy was I excited!

I gave Mr. Tomfoolery the thumbs up, but he didn't notice. He was too busy trying to hold up the weight of a giant pair of scissors. A crowd of fast food enthusiasts surrounded him on all sides. They were here for the franchise's grand opening and I had never seen anyone as fascinated with a giant ribbon as they were.

I smiled and gave Mr. Tomfoolery another thumbs up. Again, he didn't notice me. I didn't blame him. He was now really focused on cutting the ribbon with his scissors. You can say a lot of things about Mr. Tomfoolery, but you can't say he isn't a heck of a nice guy. Not only did he promote me, but he also changed his mind about using my skull as a urinal. Plus he gave me a new ear and an advance on my paycheck so I could move out of my bathroom stall and live with Stuart in his mother's house.

Outside, Mr. Tomfoolery succeeded at cutting the ribbon and the crowd let out a cheer. I gave him the thumbs up again, and I didn't care about not getting a response. I was just so proud of him.

"Monty, can you grab some empty cups from the kitchen?" El Jefe asked in his funny girl voice.

I slipped into the back before the customers stampeded through the door, although I did catch a glimpse of Stuart cutting to the front of the line.

James was in the kitchen, revealing the truth about the SECRET Malaysian government to a homeless man as he bashed his brains in with a hammer. "Oh, hi, Monty," he said. James was a friendly guy.

I gave him a thumbs up and smiled.

He frowned and looked down at the stump where his arm used to be.

Harold was standing next to Mr. Tophat, putting the finishing touches on his design. Half of the demolition derby's bronze medalist was surgically attached to the fry station, filling containers of fries for the customers, while his other half was lounging around in the cesspool beneath the Tomfoolery mansion's front yard.

He tried to eat a French fry. But before he was able to put one in his mouth, the mechanical claw grabbed it out of his hand and disappeared into the wall. Mr. Tophat made a pouty face.

Since I don't hold grudges, I had forgiven him for trying to beat me up. Attempting to lift his spirits, I gave him a thumbs up, but he was too busy frowning to notice.

Refusing to admit defeat, I gave him another one and held it until Harold tasered him into thumb-upping me back.

I loved my new job.

INTERLUDE

I call Frankie Nougat on my new cell phone. I bought it because of my anger problems and my predisposition to take out my problems on the collectible value of my *Sports Illustrated* football phone. The phone was outrageously expensive because it has many special features that cell phones that are not outrageously expensive lack. My primary reason for choosing it over a phone that was not outrageously expensive was its ability to make scrambled eggs without overcooking them. Since I am only able to do this fifty percent of the time without the assistance of an outrageously expensive cell phone, I felt it was a worthwhile investment. And it's not like I didn't have the extra money to spend—Lazy Fascist Press gave me a six figure advance to write this novel. Good thing it's a novel instead of a lame-ass novella collection or else they would have only given me a cheap vodka martini and a pink cupcake.

"Hello, you have reached Frankie Nougat's Detective Agency. We are either unavailable or on the other line."

I wonder if that freaking kid is screening his calls.

"Please leave a message after the sound of a man pretending to be murdered. And oh, if this is Mr. Sands, I want you to know I've almost cracked your case. Have a nice and mysterious day."

I hear gunshots and a man says, "Ow, oooh, eeek." My first instinct is to leave an angrily worded message. My second instinct is to throw my outrageously expensive cell phone out the window. After careful consideration, I go with my second instinct. My bedroom window shatters. My outrageously expensive cell phone falls two hundred feet. It lies on the sidewalk, unharmed. Its indestructibility is one of its many special features.

Monty Cantsin walks by the phone and looks down. He kneels to pick it up. The moment he touches it, a metal wire springs out of the phone, enters Monty's mouth, and unleashes an electronic charge. Monty Cantsin falls unconscious.

My outrageously expensive cell phone also comes equipped with a variety of anti-theft features.

I leave my apartment to recover the phone. While riding the elevator down to the street, I think of the many connections between "Frankie Nougat and the Case of the Missing Heart" and "Cheesequake Smash-Up." My brain is attacked by links between the two novellas.

"Frankie Nougat and the Case of the Missing Heart" takes place in a suburb of Cheesequake. Frankie Nougat and Bones are two of the spectators who watched the demolition derby in "Cheesequake Smash-Up." Donner Burger is Frankie Nougat's favorite fast food restaurant in "Frankie Nougat and the Case of the Missing Heart." In "Cheesequake Smash-Up," Jesus decides the winner of the demolition derby before stealing Frankie's parents' heart, which was after he stole George Lucas's heart.

I can go on like this all day, but I have an outrageously expensive cell phone to recover.

I exit my building to the street and see the phone. Next to it, Monty Cantsin flops around like a fish out of water. There is a paper bag in his left hand. I grab it.

The bag is very greasy. I open it to find a hamburger and fries. The burger smells delicious. Hunger gnaws on my stomach. I open my mouth and take a big bite.

Tastes like chicken.

That's strange. I remove the top bun. The burger patty looks like a burger patty, not chicken.

Chicken...cow. It doesn't matter which dead animal I just ate. All I know is the whatever-burger is the greatest burger I have ever eaten in my life. I take another bite.

I swallow it and ejaculate into my pants.

APOCALYPSE
NINJA

CHAPTER 1

Apocalypse Ninja's farts are silent but deadly. Apocalypse Ninja always gets shushed at the library. Apocalypse Ninja has "more to love." Apocalypse Ninja is frightened of gay people. Apocalypse Ninja is the greatest threat the china shop industry has ever known.

Apocalypse Ninja is the worst ninja ever.

CHAPTER 2

The Clan of REALLY Evil Ninjas are participating in a skydiving event in New Jersey. The event is for charity. The REALLY evil ninjas approached people on the street and "convinced" them to pledge money. The less space between the ninjas and the ground when they open their parachutes, the more money their "sponsors" will give to the charity of the ninja's choice.

The charity of the ninjas' choice is themselves. The sponsors think the ninjas' charity of choice is the homeless. The Clan of REALLY evil ninjas are crafty. The Clan of REALLY evil ninjas are REALLY evil. They participate in "charitable" events like this to convince the public they are not REALLY evil. Since ninja code has forbidden them from changing their name, they participate in a lot of "charitable" events. This is pretty much all they ever do. That, and try to bring about the apocalypse.

CHAPTER 3

Apocalypse Ninja is too afraid to skydive. He is not skydiving. He is standing on the ground among a crowd of people who think the idea of skydiving ninjas is very funny. He has misplaced his ninja outfit, so he is wearing a black trash bag. He has cut eyeholes into the trash bag so he can take advantage of his superior ninja vision. His superior ninja vision is less superior than the superior ninja vision of all the other ninjas who have existed throughout history.

Apocalypse Ninja's evil brethren are in the sky. They are in an airplane.

They are no longer in an airplane. They have jumped out. The people who think skydiving ninjas are funny are amused. They cheer.

The evil ninjas plummet toward the Earth. Some of them get a little scared. They open their parachutes. They get even more scared. Their parachutes have been replaced with skull and crossbones pirate sails. Skull and crossbones pirate sails are not as effective as parachutes. The scared ninjas fall to their deaths.

Every ninja in The Clan of REALLY Evil Ninjas have fallen to their deaths and the world is a little less evil. Every ninja in The Clan of REALLY Evil Ninjas have fallen to their deaths except Apocalypse Ninja.

Apocalypse Ninja is sad.

CHAPTER 4

A crew of pirates sit in the bleachers, cackling at their act of mass murder. Their clothing looks like it was bought at a Halloween costume shop. Manny, the first mate, wears pantaloons that seem to be made of rubber. The crew's leader, Captain Jolly Jill Rotgut, celebrates their triumph by getting up and shaking her booty. Except for Manny, the pirates do not like it when their captain shakes her booty. They do not find the captain's booty pleasant to look at when it is being shaken or engaged in any other activity. Manny does not agree. He has had a John Waters mustache and a crush on Jolly Jill since kindergarten. She has been unaware of his existence since kindergarten. Back then, her face hadn't been burnt off and she still had all of her body parts. Now most of them have been replaced by household items. She is very accident-prone. She is practically a cyborg.

Besides Manny, the crew of the Shoddy Barnacle are hiding their eyes to protect themselves from their captain's booty shaking. Besides Manny, the crew all used to be named Peter. But this was very confusing, so they legally changed their names. Unfortunately, their current names still cause mild confusion. The mildly confusing crew consists of Pete the Priapismic Pirate, Petey the Parrot Pirate, and Peter the Pacifistic Pirate. But even mildly confusing names are too complicated for the captain, so she refers to them as Erection, Cracker, and Fucking Pussy.

The crew of the Shoddy Barnacle are the worst pirates ever.

Apocalypse Ninja is an even match for the worst pirates ever.

CHAPTER 5

The clan of REALLY evil ninjas use their supernatural ninja-like abilities to come back from the dead. They whisper into Apocalypse Ninja's ear. This is their dying wish: "Make the end of the world happen. Make it happen by bringing about the second cumming of Christ."

Apocalypse Ninja thinks about what it would be like to bring about the second cumming of Christ. He says, "Ewwwww!"

Apocalypse Ninja is very homophobic. A REALLY evil ninja's penis used to creep into his bedroom as he slept. The penis would wake him up and he would be very scared. The penis made him scared of the dark. He was scared of what could be lurking in the shadows. This made Apocalypse Ninja's parents unhappy. A ninja should not be scared of what lurks in the shadows because it is ninja that lurks in the shadows.

Apocalypse Ninja's parents bought him a night light. After that, he could fall asleep again.

Apocalypse Ninja is not sure if he will ever sleep again. REALLY evil ninjas using their supernatural ninja-like abilities to come back from the dead are very scary. Apocalypse Ninja is so scared he agrees to make the end of the world happen. He tries to not think about how God's penis will feel like in his mouth.

CHAPTER 6

The pirates overhear Apocalypse Ninja's vow to make the end of the world happen. They are not happy. They like the world. Without the world, they would be unable to rape and pillage and disco dance. They attack him.

Apocalypse Ninja cries like a little girl. Apocalypse Ninja farts. Apocalypse Ninja cries and farts. The pirates know Apocalypse Ninja is crying but they do not know he is farting. They do not know he is farting because his fart did not make any noise. But his fart makes a horrible stink. His fart makes such a horrible stink that it smells worse than any fart they have ever been in the presence of. This makes the pirates confused. They try to identify the horrible stink. While they try to identify the horrible stink, Apocalypse Ninja takes off his black garbage bag ninja outfit and walks into the crowd. Without his black garbage bag ninja outfit, Apocalypse Ninja looks like everyone else. Without his black garbage bag ninja outfit, the pirates fear the end of the world is upon them.

CHAPTER 7

The REALLY evil ninjas go back to being dead because even REALLY evil ninjas do not have ultimate supernatural powers.

CHAPTER 8

Apocalypse Ninja is in a New Jersey airport. He is trying to get through security. He is trying to get through security because his ninja clan knows the secret location of Jesus Christ. The body of Jesus Christ is not located in New Jersey. It tours with a carnival. The carnival is called Jimbo Jim's Cavalcade of Exquisite Distractions. The carnival only travels through the country's Bible Belt. It is rumored to be in Oklahoma.

Apocalypse Ninja has bought himself a plane ticket. It is a first class ticket. Apocalypse Ninja was able to afford a first class ticket because The Clan of REALLY evil ninjas have left him all the money they raised with their "charitable activities."

Apocalypse Ninja is at the front of the line. The airport security man is frowning at Apocalypse Ninja's black trash bag. He is frowning at Apocalypse Ninja's ninja sword. He is frowning at Apocalypse Ninja's nunchucks. He is frowning at the collection of shuriken that are attached to Apocalypse Ninja's ninja belt. The security man says, "Sir, you'll have to remove all your weapons if you want to board the flight."

Apocalypse Ninja is very angry. He reaches for his sword. He remembers he does not know how to use his sword. He stops reaching for his sword, says, "Carrying a sword is part of my religion and if you do not let me pass you will be violating my religious rights."

The security man says, "Sir, I don't care if the relinquishment of your weapons are a violation of your religious rights. It is the policy of this airport to deny service to any passenger carrying prohibited objects."

Apocalypse Ninja gives the security man all of his weapons except his sword, says, "I need to carry around a ninja sword for medical purposes. Here is a note from my doctor."

The security man reads the "note," says, "Sir, this is not a note from your doctor. It is a tissue on which you wrote the words, 'If Apocalypse Ninja does not carry a sword then his heart condition will destroy the airport.' I'll have to ask you to leave your sword behind."

Apocalypse Ninja leaves his sword behind. This makes him sad. His mother gave him the sword for his birthday when he was six. Now his mother is dead. She died in a skydiving accident.

CHAPTER 9

The pirates gallivant on the deck of the Shoddy Barnacle as the ship rots in Horrid Harbor. Jolly Jill Rotgut puts on her hat, orders her men to sail the ship toward Oklahoma. The crew try to sail to Oklahoma. The voyage is smooth, until they hit land. The crew get out, try to carry the ship to Oklahoma. They fail. Jolly Jill Rotgut calls them little sissy men. She stares at their crotches, insults the size of their genitalia. The pirates formerly known as Peter laugh: ho ho ho ho ho.

Manny takes off his pants, stares down.

"Ho ho ho ho ho," the other pirates laugh

Manny thinks they are laughing at his genitalia, not with his genitalia. He cries. He tries to put his pants back on, but has a tough time doing it. Pirate pants are tricky. Easier to take off than put on. He keeps having a tough time and he keeps crying and the pirates keep laughing. Ho ho ho ho ho.

CHAPTER 10

Apocalypse Ninja is sitting in first class, preparing for takeoff. He always prepares for takeoff by hyperventilating. Apocalypse Ninja is afraid of flying, but not as much as he is afraid of homosexuals.

Scarlett Johansson is unhappy. She does not like sitting next to a hyperventilating ninja in a trash bag. She taps Apocalypse Ninja on the shoulder, says, "Stop, you're making me uncomfortable."

Apocalypse Ninja stops hyperventilating. He ogles Scarlett Johansson, says, "Hey, babe. I love your boobs. They're sooo nice. Even bigger than my mom's, and she's dead. Ever wanted to touch ninja penis? I know I have!" Punches himself in the face. "Crap! Just kidding! I really am! You've gotta believe me!" Looking sly, he takes out a small pair of scissors and trims his nose hair. "So you wanna see if we can both fit in the bathroom—without clothes!—or what?"

Scarlett Johansson presses the call button. A stewardess comes over. Scarlett Johansson says, "I would like to change seats please." The stewardess says, "Yes, Miss Johansson."

Scarlett Johansson changes her seat.

CHAPTER 11

Captain Jolly Jill Rotgut gave up on the idea of sailing to Oklahoma, so the pirates now sit in economy class on an airplane. It takes off. The captain experiences anal tremors. She always experiences anal tremors during takeoff. This is why she chose an exciting career as a pirate captain rather than an airplane pilot.

The pirates formerly known as Peter are experiencing back pain. The seats are very uncomfortable. There is hardly any room to stretch their legs. A baby is showing her affection for Manny by spitting at him and giggling. He presses the call button. A stewardess does not come over to assist him. He presses the call button again, waits ten minutes, removes a skull and crossbones bandana from his pocket to wipe off the spittle, opens his mouth to call the stewardess. The baby spits a gob of phlegm down his throat.

The curtain in the front of the plane opens. The pirates see Apocalypse Ninja sitting in a comfortable seat, drinking champagne with his arm around a beautiful redhead. Captain Jolly Jill Rotgut removes her seatbelt, yells, "First man to bring me his head gets a gift certificate to Amazon.com!"

CHAPTER 12

The beautiful redhead who exchanged seats with Scarlett Johansson is very beautiful. The beautiful redhead is very drunk. She has drunk enough doll-sized liquor bottles to fill a gumball machine. She doesn't know Apocalypse Ninja's arm is around her. She doesn't know she is flying six miles above the ground.

Manny goes to the bathroom. Jolly Jill Rotgut and the pirates formerly known as Peter break through the barrier between first class and economy class. Well-to-do passengers are offended by their decrepit clothing, pungent odors, and bad posture. They all press their call buttons at the same time, resulting in a temporary loss of power, a near-fatal freefall, and prayers to many gods.

The pirates pick themselves off the floor, stumble toward Apocalypse Ninja. An army of stewardesses block their path. The head stewardess is a female bodybuilding champion. Her name is Arnold Schwarzenegger. Steroids pump through her veins. Bodybuilding competition judges are afraid to give her a drug test. The judges are afraid she will squeeze their heads until they burst. She says, "I need to see your tickets."

Jolly Jill Rotgut knows what will happen if they show Arnold Schwarzenegger their tickets. Arnold Schwarzenegger will say, "I'm sorry. You're not supposed to be here. Please go back to your seats." Then she will flex and put on a scary face.

Jolly Jill Rotgut says, "We left our tickets in our anal

cavities." She buries her face in her tong-hands. She is so ashamed. Why did she say that? Was it really the best way out of their predicament? She was a little nervous. Arnold Schwarzenegger makes her nervous.

The head stewardess flexes, puts on a scary face, says, "I'm going to have to ask you to locate your tickets. We have a washroom located on the other side of the plane that's available for this purpose."

Jolly Jill Rotgut considers continuing with the anal cavity charade. Should she tell the truth? No, she is a pirate captain. Pirate captains do not tell the truth. Pirate captains lie and pillage and destroy. She will lie to Arnold Schwarzenegger, pillage the first class section, destroy her and the other stewardesses.

She yells, "Attack!"

CHAPTER 13

Cracker the Parrot Pirate flies around with a knife between his teeth. It is a tiny knife, a plastic knife, the kind of knife that's so cute it makes airport security go awwwww.

Arnold Schwarzenegger addresses the Captain with an "Excuse me, miss, but your animal should have been stored in our pet center, which is located in the cargo hold."

Cracker says, "Raaaar. I'm a pirate, not a pet. Raaaar." He swoops down on Arnold Schwarzenegger's shoulder, tries to slit her throat. Arnold Schwarzenegger says, "awwwww."

Jolly Jill Rotgut reveals her battle cry—skinna-ma-rinky-dinky-doo!—and attacks Arnold Schwarzenegger with one of the household items she uses as a weapon.

Arnold Schwarzenegger says, "Excuse me, miss, but will you stop grabbing my uniform with your tongs?" She does not notice Erection, who is chasing the other stewardesses around the compartment as he waves his penis like a cutlass.

Fucking Pussy believes non-violent resistance is the best policy, and he acts accordingly—by putting his hands over his head and lying down on the floor.

Arnold Schwarzenegger notices what Erection is doing. She stops lecturing Jolly Jill Rotgut on the impoliteness of grabbing a world champion bodybuilder's stewardess uniform and lunges at Erection, knocking over many stewardesses. Then she confiscates Apocalypse Ninja's champagne glass and breaks it over Erection's head.

Manny comes out of the bathroom and asks Apocalypse

Ninja to reconsider the nature of his quest.

Jolly Jill Rotgut tries to remove Arnold Schwarzenegger's left eye.

Apocalypse Ninja looks at Manny and holds out his hand, curling his fingers into the shape of a cup. Says, "I want a refill."

Arnold Schwarzenegger punches Jolly Jill Rotgut in the nose. It rolls off, hits the floor. Arnold Schwarzenegger stares at the nose, says, "Oh my God! I'm so sorry!" She notices the nose is not a nose. It is a golf ball. She looks at her bloody knuckles, takes Jolly Jill Rotgut's head in one hand and Erection's head in the other. Smashes them together. Says something to a stewardess who is short and fat. The stewardess leaves.

Manny says, "Sorry, but I'm a pirate, not a stewardess. But you should still pay attention to what I've got to say. Listen, Apocalypse Ninja, the end of the world is really bad. Stop trying to destroy the planet."

Apocalypse Ninja says, "I want a refill."

Manny is frustrated.

The short, fat stewardess comes back with two zip ties and a cage. She hands the zip ties to Arnold Schwarzenegger, leaves the cage on the floor. Arnold Schwarzenegger pulls Jolly Jill's tong-hands behind her back, ties the zips around them like handcuffs. She does the same to Erection. Then she picks up the cage, opens it, and chases Cracker around the compartment until she catches him inside the cage. "Petey wants freedom from confined spaces," he squeaks. Arnold Schwarzenegger escorts Jolly Jill and Erection to a holding cell, Cracker to the pet center. On her way, she steps on Fucking Pussy's back. His bones crunch, but she does not hear them make a sound.

CHAPTER 14

The plane lands. Apocalypse Ninja leans over, vomits on the beautiful redhead's lap. She does not notice. Today is not her day for noticing the details. Apocalypse Ninja is a little embarrassed, but not much. He whispers into her ear, "I love you, beautiful redhead. Your boobs aren't bigger than my dead mom's but they're still very nice. Thanks for letting me use your hands like they were my puppets. Tell them thanks for participating in a puppet show where they touched my ninja penis. I bet they have always wanted to do that. Sorry about the puke." He stands up, leaves the airplane, walks through the gate and sees the beautiful Oklahoma sky through the airport's glass windows.

CHAPTER 15

Air marshals escort Jolly Jill Rotgut and Erection off the plane. They use the back exit. They do not want to cause the other passengers to feel uncomfortable. It is against airline policy. Jolly Jill and Fucking Pussy do not have to wait twenty minutes to get off the plane like Manny.

Manny waits twenty minutes to get off the plane. He gets off the plane.

The short, fat stewardess carries Cracker in his cage. She brings him to the airport's pet pickup location. No one picks him up.

Jolly Jill Rotgut and Erection are brought to a police station. The air marshals fill out paperwork and leave them in the custody of the police, who confiscate their belts and bootlaces and lock them in a holding cell. The police do not want to be liable for any hangings in the holding cell. Sometimes people get sad in holding cells and want a quick and easy solution for ending their sadness. But Jolly Jill and Erection are not sad. They are annoyed. They are annoyed that their pants are falling down. They are annoyed at the looseness of their boots. They are used to tight boots and pants that stay up. These things bring them comfort.

Back at the airport, Fucking Pussy is still on the floor of the plane. Many of his bones are broken. He wishes he had some really nice painkillers. An airplane cleaning person walks over him. He yelps. The cleaning person stops, looks down, does not know where Fucking Pussy's yelp came from. The pirate says, "Help, I need medical assistance."

The cleaning person remains confused. Fucking Pussy spits in the cleaning person's face, repeats himself. The cleaning person is no longer confused. He kicks the pirate in the ear, radios for medical assistance.

CHAPTER 16

Jolly Jill Rotgut and Erection sing sea shanties to pass the time.

CHAPTER 17

Apocalypse Ninja walks through a small town. The residents eye him with suspicion. Apocalypse Ninja has a strut to his walk. He thinks it makes him look suave. It does not. It makes him look like he has suffered nerve damage to his brain.

He goes into a gas station, says, "What up, nigga?" and asks the cashier for directions to Jimbo Jim's Carnival of Exquisite Distractions.

The cashier is startled. The cashier is a sixty-year-old white male. No one has called him a nigga before. He wonders if he should be outraged. A ninja has never asked him for directions before. He has come in contact with a lot of ninjas during his life, but they always seemed to know where they were going. Ninjas are not known for asking for directions at gas stations. The cashier decides to be outraged, says, "Get the holy heck out of here!"

Apocalypse Ninja is scared. The man has made him this way. His voice was very loud. He does not like it when people have loud voices. It makes him scared. It makes him want to leave.

Apocalypse Ninja leaves.

CHAPTER 18

While in the airport's pet pickup location, Cracker shoves his talon through his cage and opens the door. He is able to escape because he is a pirate, not a pet. He flies to the nearest ice cream parlor. This is where the crew of the Shoddy Barnacle are supposed to meet if they get separated. Jolly Jill Rotgut chose the nearest ice cream parlor as a meeting place because she really likes Chunky Monkey.

Cracker lands at The Oklahoma Ice Cream Extravaganza, sees Manny eating a vanilla ice cream cone with sprinkles. The parrot tries to tell him Jolly Jill Rotgut and Erection were arrested, but Manny refuses to listen until he finishes his cone. He is really enjoying it and doesn't want bad news about his beloved to ruin its flavor. He also might be the slowest ice cream eater known to piratekind.

After one hour and twelve minutes, Manny has successfully slurped up all the melted ice cream. He raises his hat to indicate he is prepared to hear the bad news.

Cracker tells him the news. Manny sighs with regret. The two pirates plan a rescue.

CHAPTER 19

Fucking Pussy lies in a hospital bed with many broken bones. Casts and bandages cover his entire body. He looks a little like a mummy. A funny mummy, which is what little children call him as they pass by his corner of the uninsured ward. He is tired at being laughed at by little children and anxious to escape from the hospital before he needs to pay his bill so he can rescue his crewmates.

He flags down an old man in a wheelchair, struggles out of bed, bashes the man in the nose with his arm cast, and steals his wheelchair. He rolls himself out of the hospital with security in pursuit.

CHAPTER 20

While searching for Jimbo Jim's Carnival of Exquisite Distractions, Apocalypse Ninja finds a gun store. He walks inside—hoping to replace the weapons that airport security confiscated from him—and asks the store owner for assistance.

The owner says, "We don't carry no goddamn ninja swords in this establishment."

Apocalypse Ninja frowns, scans the walls of the shop. He sees hundreds of guns. This does not please him. He does not know how to shoot a gun. None of the guns even look like a ninja sword.

"Do you sell nunchucks?" he asks. "Shuriken?"

The store owner says, "Nope and nope." He looks frustrated.

So Apocalypse Ninja buys himself a gun.

CHAPTER 21

Cracker and Manny meet Fucking Pussy in front of the police station where Jolly Jill Rotgut and Erection are being held. They cackle at his mummy-like appearance, then break their crewmates out. They do this by impersonating police officers and slitting any throats that get in their way with the small glass daggers they smuggled through airport security in their jockstraps.

CHAPTER 22

Apocalypse Ninja brings his gun to the state fair. He does not know it is the state fair. It was a few blocks away from the gun store and he thinks it is Jimbo Jim's Cavalcade of Exquisite Distraction. Since he loves fried dough, he goes to the fried dough booth, where he is not asked to pay.

While Apocalypse Ninja munches on the dough, a man in a cowboy hat shouts, "Try your luck! Knock all the cans down and win a timeshare in the Bahamas!"

Apocalypse Ninja does not want to try his luck. He does not want to win a timeshare in the Bahamas. But he thinks the man can tell him where to find the body of Jesus Christ.

He walks over to the booth, wolfs down the rest of the dough, stares at the pyramid of cans. It glistens. He forgets about the body of Christ. He is engrossed in the cans, in his desire to knock them down and win a timeshare in the Bahamas. He starts shooting. The man with the cowboy hat squeals, takes cover. Bullets hit many things, but they do not hit the cans. Apocalypse Ninja feels ashamed. He opens his fanny pack, reaches for more bullets.

The man with the cowboy hat shouts, "Congratulations, you're a winner!" and shoves a stuffed hippo into Apocalypse Ninja's arms. Then he gives him an inflatable heart and a big pen and a dinosaur-shaped balloon and a calculator and a giant Reese's Peanut Butter Cup...

Apocalypse Ninja has a lot of trouble holding all his prizes at the same time, but he tries his best. He does not want to seem impolite.

...and a crocodile made of confetti and giant-sized punching gloves and a talking clock and a big hammer made of plastic and a scary mask and a pink pocketbook and a smiling skeleton and a...

CHAPTER 23

The pirates are arguing in the parking lot of the police station. They need a getaway vehicle, because they need to get away. They need to do this because they have murdered a station-full of police officers, which is against the law.

The pirates formerly known as Peter want to steal a police car. "It will be very easy," Fucking Pussy says. "We can go through one of the police officer's pockets, find his keys, and try them in every car on the lot. Twenty minutes tops."

Jolly Jill Rotgut and Manny are against stealing a police car. Jolly Jill Rotgut wants to escape in a pirate ship. She thinks pirates look stupid while driving in police cars. She does not like to look stupid. She already looks pretty stupid considering most of her body parts have been replaced by household items. Manny agrees with her about wanting to escape in a pirate ship because he is a kiss-ass.

Cracker says, "Raaaar. What if we made a police car look like a pirate ship? Raaaar."

Jolly Jill Rotgut is ok with this idea, and so is Manny. She rifles through the pockets of a dead police officer, finds his keys, tries them in almost every car in the lot. After twenty minutes, she finds the correct car and celebrates by pumping her tongs in the air. Then the crew drive to Wal-Mart for supplies, glue pieces of shoplifted wood across the car's exterior, use white spray paint to make a Jolly Roger out of a black piece of fabric, and hoist it over the roof.

They get into the pirate ship police car, drive down the

street. They look really stupid. It would have looked less stupid if they had not disguised the police car as a pirate ship. Jill Rotgut does not realize this. She thinks they look cool. She drives with one tong-hand, swinging a bottle of Vitamin Water she bought from the police station's Vitamin Water machine in the other while singing a sea shanty about drinking grog. She swallows a big gulp of it, thinking it is cool to pretend that a bottle of Vitamin Water is grog.

CHAPTER 24

The pirates are unable to escape from town. The state fair is blocking the road, so the crew get out of their pirate ship police car and go on foot.

Manny is nervous. He is worried about being arrested by the police officers who are still living. Why couldn't they have been answering phones at the station rather than giving speeding tickets and responding to domestic abuse calls? He is angry at these police officers for not making themselves easy targets. *We should be wearing disguises*, he thinks. *Pirates stand out too much in a crowd.* "We should be dressed as unemployed television enthusiasts," he tells Jolly Jill, but she does not know he exists.

Erection spots Apocalypse Ninja, yells, "There he is!"

CHAPTER 25

Apocalypse Ninja is tired of being polite to the man with the cowboy hat. He is starting to give him the same prizes twice, sometimes three times. Apocalypse Ninja says, "That's enough, thank you." But the man keeps piling the prizes into his arms. Eventually, there are so many prizes that Apocalypse Ninja is forced to throw his gun down on the ground.

It goes off, and a bullet pierces the man's cowboy hat. He takes it off, looks at the hole, opens his mouth to release a silent scream. Calmly, he puts his hat back on, picks up Apocalypse Ninja's gun, points it at him, says, "Give me back my goddamn merchandise, freako."

While Apocalypse Ninja is dropping his prizes onto the counter, Jolly Jill Rotgut sneaks up behind him, rubs her tongs against her neck, says, "One move and you die."

Apocalypse Ninja looks down, says, "Are those...tongs?" He has a giggle fit.

An expression of contempt crosses Jolly Jill's face as she watches Apocalypse Ninja's titties shake. Insulted, she grabs his neck with her tongs. He laughs even louder. Her "weapon" has no effect on him. Apocalypse Ninja is totally invincible.

She releases him, points her tongs at Fucking Pussy, says, "You! Kill him! Now!"

The pirate hobbles toward Apocalypse Ninja, goes to shake his hand. He says, "Hi, my name is Peter the Pacifistic Pirate. It's really nice to meet you."

Apocalypse Ninja shakes back, says, "Hey, man. I'm Apocalypse Ninja. Are you a mummy?"

Fucking Pussy ignores his question, says, "So listen—let's be friends. We can do lots of social activities together, like hanging out, engaging in male bonding experiences, and not destroying the world by bringing about the second cumming of Christ. How does that sound?"

"Sorry, dog. I promised and shit. You wanna hit a strip club or something?"

Erection says, "No, but thanks for offering. Strip clubs aren't really my thing. They objectify women."

"Your loss," Apocalypse Ninja says, then he moves his tongue rapidly, pretending the air is a tasty vagina.

Furious, Jolly Jill Rotgut tries to destroy the can-shooting booth with her skull. She stops, says, "Oww," rubs her head, says, "Will somebody just kill him?"

Cracker perches down on Apocalypse Ninja's shoulder, tries to slice through his neck with his little plastic knife. Apocalypse Ninja has another giggle fit. He holds his breath, counts to ten, says, "Polly want an Indonesian hooker?"

Erection lunges at Apocalypse Ninja, waving his glass dagger. The man with the cowboy hat points the gun at the pirate's pecker, says, "I've had enough of y'all. Get outta here or I'm blowin' it off."

Apocalypse Ninja feels empathy for another man's penis. If the penis were in his own pants, he would not want it to be destroyed, so he moves away from the booth.

Fucking Pussy catches up to him, says, "Hello, Apocalypse Ninja, my friend. I have an idea. A pie eating contest is coming up soon. We should compete against each other. If I win, you'll stop trying to destroy the world. And if you win, I'll give you my slutty cousin's phone number. How does that sound?"

"I'm in," Apocalypse Ninja says, looking forward to

asking Fucking Pussy's slutty cousin what she *isn't* wearing, looking forward to annihilating this skinny pirate wimp, looking forward to eating.

CHAPTER 26

Apocalypse Ninja sits on stage behind a long table. He looks down at a pumpkin pie, salivates. Fucking Pussy is sitting on the other side of the table. Fat men sit between them. They are much fatter than Apocalypse Ninja. He makes fun of them in his mind.

A man in a hippopotamus costume says, "Ready, set, go!" and fires a starter pistol. Apocalypse Ninja devours his first pie in three seconds. Fucking Pussy takes slow, deliberate bites. He has a strategy to win: he will take his time to eat. There will be a point in the competition when Apocalypse Ninja is either too nauseous to continue or too nauseous to avoid vomiting. If he does not vomit, Fucking Pussy will catch up to him, eating slowly and steadily, and ultimately defeat him. If Apocalypse Ninja vomits, he will be disqualified, and the pirate can stop eating, knowing he does not have to win the competition to beat Apocalypse Ninja.

Fucking Pussy cannot lose.

CHAPTER 27

Eight policemen in riot gear show up while Apocalypse Ninja is eating a chocolate cream pie. This is unfortunate. Chocolate cream is Apocalypse Ninja's favorite.

One of the police officers speaks through a megaphone: "Stop eating those pies. The pie eating contest is over."

The crowd groans.

"I repeat—the pie eating contest is over." He reads off a list of names: "Captain Jill Rotgut, Pete the Priapismic Pirate, Petey the Parrot Pirate, Peter the Pacifistic Pirate, and…uh… Manny—throw down your weapons and put your hands up. You are under arrest for multiple homicides." He whispers under his breath, "And I will fucking eat your souls."

Fucking Pussy drops his glass dagger, feels regret. He went through a lot of pain for that dagger. It stabbed his scrotum hundreds of times while going through airport security. Now he will never get to use it. He was looking forward to using it for pacifistic purposes, like if Apocalypse Ninja tied up one of his crewmates with a really tricky knot and they needed a sharp dagger to escape.

Now I will never experience true glory, he thinks while two police officers beat the shit out of him.

CHAPTER 28

Jolly Jill Rotgut is surrounded. Guns are aimed at her head. An officer says, "Drop your weapons."

She has no choice, so she obeys. She drops her tongs, leaf blower, micro fridge, juicer, and clock radio. The police officers gasp at her appearance. If she had not chosen an exciting career as a pirate captain, she could have worked at Jimbo Jim's Cavalcade of Exquisite Distractions as The Human Torso.

Apocalypse Ninja taps her on the shoulder, says, "I'll take care of this, hot stuff. Cover your nose." She scoffs at him. He yells, "Do it!" A police officer wraps his hands around her neck, squeezes. She has second thoughts, covers her nose. Apocalypse Ninja lifts up his black trash bag ninja outfit, pulls down his sweat pants and his Spiderman underoos. He farts, silent and extremely fucking deadly. Everyone in the vicinity who is not Jolly Jill faint from the stench. Mist covers the landscape, looking like fog from a machine at a heavy metal concert. Apocalypse Ninja carries Jolly Jill over to a pigpen, holds her face-first over the feces, and rubs her nose in it. She gags. He says, "I know it smells bad, but it's the only thing keeping you conscious." She gets used to the stench. Apocalypse Ninja rolls Jolly Jill in a wheelbarrow, goes back to her pile of household items. The two adversaries reattach them, then locate each of the captain's unconscious crewmembers and pile them in the wheelbarrow. There is some confusion in regards to Manny when Jolly Jill Rotgut insists he is an invisible person who is not a member of her crew, but Apocalypse Ninja perseveres and puts him in the wheelbarrow. They go behind a tent where the police will not find them.

Jolly Jill Rotgut smiles at Apocalypse Ninja underneath a mustache of pig shit, says, "Thank you."

Apocalypse Ninja smiles back, hits her in the face with a two-by-four.

"This is what you get," he says, hitting her again. "This is what you get when you fuck with Apocalypse Ninja." When her face has collapsed into itself and he is sure she is dead, he stops hitting her.

He turns the wheelbarrow over. Jolly Jill's crewmembers fall on the ground. Apocalypse Ninja takes turns hitting each of them until their faces have collapsed and he is sure they are dead.

Apocalypse Ninja may lack skills in the martial arts, but like most people, he is a competent wielder of the two-by-four.

CHAPTER 29

Apocalypse Ninja does a victory dance. It is The Running Man. It is...

Awesome.

While Apocalypse Ninja is doing a victory dance and looking awesome, Jolly Jill defies his ability to tell the difference between the living and the dead by kicking him in the testicles with her mini fridge. Then she removes her magical ray gun from her ribcage and shoots him, causing his body to transform into particles and seep into the beautiful Oklahoma sky.

CHAPTER 30

Apocalypse Ninja wakes up in a jungle. He is naked. He has an aching pain in his groin. He is crying like a eunuch.

"Where am I?" he squeals.

Monkeys swoop down from the trees, contort their bodies to form the word "Zimbabwe."

"Holy crap!" he says. He stares down at his swollen gonads, thinks, *How will I destroy the world with balls this huge?* How will I destroy the world when I'm a prisoner of Zimbabwe? He looks around at the lush vegetation and exotic animals, says, "Zimbabwe fucking sucks," vomits, and passes out.

CHAPTER 31

The pirates trudge through the fairground, horrifying obese children with their mangled faces. A police officer eyes them suspiciously, and Jolly Jill hurries them along.

Erection asks, "How will we get out of town without getting busted?" It hurts to speak.

Jolly Jill Rotgut says, "I saw a ski shop on the way to Wal-Mart. We can buy ski masks and wear them to cover our faces. The cops won't have a clue."

Cracker says, "Raaaar, we don't need ski masks. Apocalypse Ninja beat our faces beyond recognition, raaaar."

Jolly Jill says, "That kind of talk will get us caught. We're buying ski masks, and that's the end of it. I'm your captain. Anybody who argues with me gets keelhauled."

Cracker says, "Raaaar."

She snarls, "It's keelhauling time for you, parrot!"

Manny wishes Jolly Jill Rotgut knew he existed.

CHAPTER 32

"Waaaaake uuuup!" sings a voice in the key of falsetto.

Apocalypse Ninja opens his eyes. He is lying in bed, still naked. A six-foot-tall guy with long, blond hair kneels in front of him. He is wearing tight leather pants and an unbuttoned jean jacket. His shaved potbelly peeks through the jacket. There is a microphone in his hand, pressed to his lips. Apocalypse Ninja thinks, *This shit is really gay*, closes his eyes, goes back to sleep.

"Waaaaake uuuup!"

Apocalypse Ninja wakes up, rubs his sore testicles, asks, "Where am I?"

The guy sings, "Ziiiiimbaaaaabwayyyy."

Apocalypse Ninja says, "I knew that. The monkeys told me."

"The monkeys, huh?" the guy says, putting on a phony smile.

Apocalypse Ninja asks, "So where in Zimbabwe am I?"

"You've been crashing at The World Headquarters of Meeeeeetal."

Apocalypse Ninja looks around, sees a couple of dirty couches, a table with an ashtray with cigarette butts spilling out of it, a bunch of empty cans of Bud Light, a drum set, walls covered by posters with big-haired women in lingerie, and a guitar that is glued to the ceiling. He says, "This doesn't look like The World Headquarters of Metal. It looks more like my room in my dead parents' basement."

"This is definitely The World Headquarter of Meeeeeetal.

It's home to the world's greatest meeeeeetal band: The Glam Toasters."

Apocalypse Ninja says, "Never heard of them."

The guy looks like he is about to cry, then regains his composure. "Everybody's heard of The Glam Toasters. You must have crashed into the jungle when you were a baby. Your parents died, but you survived and all the jungle animals adopted you as their own child. And you've been living in the jungle ever since. Yeah, dude, that's what must have happened. The reason why you're naked and never heard of The Glam Toasters."

"I already told you, man, I live in my parents' basement."

A tear falls down the guy's cheek. "Is it a jungle basement?" he asks.

"No, it's not a jungle basement."

"Nah, dude, it's a jungle basement," he says, swinging his hair out of his eyes. "That's cool. Jungle basements are pure meeeeeetal and meeeeeetal will live forever!"

"Whatever you say, man"

The guy hands Apocalypse Ninja a signed glossy photo of himself, says, "I'm pumped to meet you, jungle dude. I'm Dickie, lead singer of The Glam Toasters, the world's greatest meeeeeetal band. We found you passed out in a puddle of vomit. Figured you could use a Bud Light."

Apocalypse Ninja accepts the photo, tells Dickie he needs to escape from Zimbabwe.

"Why do you want to leave Zimbabwe?" Dickie asks. "Zimbabwe is wicked. The Glam Toasters are huuuuge in Zimbabwe. After our American record label dropped us, we moved to a country that cared about meeeeeetal."

"I promised to destroy the world and I can only do that from the United States."

"Gotcha, dude. The apocalypse is pure meeeeeetal. The

Glam Toasters are gonna help you get out of Zimbabwe."
He takes a deep breath, then shatters Apocalypse Ninja's
eardrums with his high-pitched vocal stylings: "Glaaaam
Toaoaoaoasters assemble!"

CHAPTER 33

Cracker flies behind the pirate ship police car as the rest of the crew drive away from the fair. A piece of string is tied around his talon. The other end is attached to the ship-car's bumper. Jolly Jill Rotgut keeps looking back at the parrot and giving him the finger. She is angry at his ability to fly. She had intended to drag him. She wanted him to suffer pain, to pay for questioning her authority, but he is neither suffering nor paying. Instead, he is whistling at roadkill and counting the number of station wagons that pass by.

Jolly Jill Rotgut throws a stale donut at his head, misses.

CHAPTER 34

A bunch of middle-aged guys who shouldn't be wearing tight clothes (but are) surround Apocalypse Ninja. Their heads are covered in a mixture of bald spots and long strands of hair. Dickie says, "Ok, gang, we're gonna help this naked dude conjure Satan with our meeeeeetal and get the Prince of Darkness to bring on the Apocalyyyyypse!"

The middle-aged guys bang their heads, pump their fists, say, "Oh, yeah!"

Apocalypse Ninja says, "No, no. I don't need Satan to destroy the Earth. I need Jesus."

The guys look disappointed, hug themselves.

Apocalypse Ninja starts to get out of bed, says, "Thanks for everything, but I've really got to go." Then he yelps, rubs his testicles.

Dickie says, "Dude, you're not going anywhere with those giant swollen testicles. Don't worry. The Glam Toasters will nurse you back to health. Ready, guys?"

The middle-aged guys scramble around the room, open closets, remove instruments, plug wires into the walls, attack their hairdos with cans of hairspray, light their farts on fire with matches and hairspray, chuckle, notice they have burnt holes in their leather pants, whine, recover their composure, pose with their instruments, let it loose.

Dickie sings:

Try to grow breasts

But you're only a man
And a man's gotta learn to fake it

Try to believe
Though you aren't lactating
That you gotta tweak your nipples to make it

Apocalypse Ninja gives Dickie a "What the hell?" look. Dickie gives him a "Just trust me," look, throws him a tube of ointment, and makes the universal sign for rubbing ointment on your testicles.

You can afford silicone injections
Try and you'll grow into double D's

Never doubt that you can grow breasts
And you can attain your dreams!

The middle-aged guys shout, "Oh yeah!" Apocalypse Ninja hesitates about using the ointment in front of a bunch of dudes, but his testicles really hurt.

Grow breasts!
Shop around!
Being poor's never gonna keep you down
Grow breasts!
Shop around!
Being poor's never gonna keep you dow-ow-ow-ow-own

Apocalypse Ninja conquers his inhibitions, rubs the ointment on his testicles, feels relief.

Seek a plastic surgeon 'til the end

Cause your sex appeal will depend
On the female hormones you have inside you

Ah you gotta feel around
Tryin' to milk your own mound
When the laws in the reality fight against you

Try your best
And you'll soon be lying in the sun
With twenty pounds of fun
Wrapped inside a tiny bikini

Apocalypse Ninja gets out of bed, jumps and jump and jumps. His testicles bob up and down. They no longer hurt him.

Grow breasts!
Shop around!
Being poor's never gonna keep you down
Grow breasts!
Shop around!
Being poor's never gonna keep you dow-ow-ow-ho-how-ho-own

One of the middle-aged guys plays a guitar solo. It is inspiring. Even with all the middle-aged guys around, Apocalypse Ninja is inspired to put his penis in his hand and start pumping.

Beg for money 'til you drop
Never stop
Cause it's not over
Til you've got the best rack in tow-owwwn

Grow breasts!
Shop around!

Being poor's never gonna keep you down
Grow breasts!
Shop!
Around!

Apocalypse Ninja ejaculates, releases a flash flood of semen. It splatters all over the ceiling. His testicles shrivel back to their normal size. He can feel no pain.

CHAPTER 35

The pirates arrive at the ski shop, try to buy masks with doubloons. The coins are not accepted, so they pay with an American Express card. It is rejected.

Jolly Jill Rotgut knocks the cashier unconscious with her good fist, steals the masks, runs out. Her men follow. She distributes the masks, says, "Wait, I forgot my change," goes back for contents of the cash register. There is a lot of it. She does not like to keep a lot of cash on her person. She goes back outside, puts on her mask. Her men follow suit. They get in the pirate ship police car, drive to the bank. Jolly Jill Rotgut goes inside to make a deposit. The others follow because it is boring to wait in the car.

CHAPTER 36

Apocalypse Ninja is wearing an extra extra extra extra extra large Glam Toasters t-shirt. It is swimming on him, but that's the point. The band did not want to give him pants. All their pants are leather and expensive. They did not want to give away something so luxurious. He is wearing an extra extra extra extra extra large Glam Toasters t-shirt to avoid being arrested for indecent exposure. "I'm ready to escape from Zimbabwe," he says. "How the fuck am I going to escape from Zimbabwe?"

Dickie says, "You can do aaaaanything with the power of meeeeeetal."

"That's a bunch of bullshit."

"Nah-ah. All you need to do is to think of a place and the power of meeeeeetal will bring you there. It's like the transporter beam in Star Trek, but more badass."

CHAPTER 37

"Hi, I would like to make a deposit."

"Oh my god! It's a robbery!"

"Where?"

"I'll give you anything you want. Just don't hurt anybody."

"I wanna give you things. I'm not interested in anything you have. And I don't feel like hurting anyone. Hurting people is fun, but I'm tired. Can't I ever get a freakin' break?"

Then the shooting starts.

CHAPTER 38

And the shooting stops when Cracker pecks out the security guard's eyeballs.

Jolly Jill Rotgut runs out of the bank, regretting she doesn't have time to watch the security guard blubber over his detached eyeballs and give them little kisses. Her men follow her into the pirate ship police car.

After driving for a couple of minutes, they hear sirens and a "Pull over immediately!" Jolly Jill turns around, sees many police cars on their tail, cackles. She loves exciting sea battles, thinks this is a sea battle instead of a high speed chase. Sometimes she gets a little nutty in the head—confusing reality with the pirate's life—especially when she forgets to take her pills, and she left them back in her medicine cabinet on the Shoddy Barnacle. "Fire off the cannons, men!"

Used to accommodating their captain's delusions, the crew make cannon sounds with the back of their throats.

"Ah!" she says, "A direct hit! We showed those scallywags what we're made out of." She picks up her good arm and wiggles her arm fat, says, "Jell-O gelatin."

She takes her eyes off the road to stare at her arm fat and grins. Then the pirate ship police car crashes into the mouth of a cave.

CHAPTER 39

The power of metal transports Apocalypse Ninja to Jimbo Jim's Cavalcade of Exquisite Distractions.

CHAPTER 40

Jimbo Jim is barking, but not like a dog: "Step right up and experience anomalies and curiosities like you've never seen before. You will be dazzled by The Clean-Shaved Lady— never has a carnival dared to present a specimen like this before. You will be wowed by Zeus, a corpse who hasn't shown his age in thousands of years. You will be astounded by Mysterio the Moving Cave's inclination to follow us around wherever we may go. Step right up and enter Jimbo Jim's Cavalcade of Exquisite Distractions. The mysteries of mass media culture await you inside."

CHAPTER 41

"Uh...hi," a man with funny shorts says to the pirates. "You're not supposed to be inside our cave because you haven't paid the admission fees."

Jolly Jill Rotgut says, "We left our tickets in our anal cavities."

"Yeah...we get that excuse a lot. I know you haven't paid. I watched your...uh...thing crash and flip over. You didn't have time to pay the fee. You were too busy crashing and flipping. But I'd like to take this moment to offer you a once in a lifetime opportunity. Pay only nineteen ninety-nine per person and you will be shocked and awed by the wonders of Jimbo Jim's Cavalcade of Exquisite Distractions...at least until closing."

Jolly Jill says, "Arrrrrrr, sounds like a fair price, but I'm having a little trouble getting to my money. This isn't really a convenient time, being trapped in this pirate ship and all, metal debris wrapped around my body, baking in unholy fire. I think this pirate ship is about to explode."

"Oh, *right*," says the man with funny shorts. He leaves the cave, comes back a few minutes later with a buzz saw, cuts Jolly Jill and her crew out of the wreck, takes out a calculator, adds up some figures, says, "Now how about that ninety-nine dollars and ninety-five cents?"

That does not seem correct to Jolly Jill. She loses herself in thought, says, "That should only be $79.76. There are only three crew members besides myself."

The man says, "No, there's four."

Manny forks over his admission fee. Jolly Jill Rotgut says, "I'm only paying for three, you cheating scum suckling scabies scab."

The man nods in agreement.

She counts eighty dollars out of the loot from the ski shop, asks for change.

The man with funny shorts searches through his pockets for a nickel. It takes him about ten minutes and Jolly Jill displays an unusual degree of patience. After he hands it to her, they sprint out of the cave and the pirate ship police car explodes. A fireball shoots out of the cave's mouth, throwing them into the air.

They fall back down, landing on The World's Largest Watermelon.

CHAPTER 42

Apocalypse Ninja hears the sound of an explosion. He is not the least bit interested in its source. He is too busy watching The Three Titty Review inside a tent. If he is to complete his mission by totally fagging out, he wants to go into it knowing he has proven his masculinity by watching a group of three-breasted women do The Macarena while in their bikinis.

One of the three-breasted women has a wardrobe malfunction. Her middle breast falls out. Apocalypse Ninja hoots, stomps his feet, chants, "USA! USA!" He feels like the most heterosexual ninja on Earth.

CHAPTER 43

Jolly Jill Rotgut's hat is on fire. She and her crew are covered in watermelon. They feel sticky, uncomfortable. They do not appreciate it when Jimbo Jim yells in their faces. He gets really close to Jolly Jill Rotgut's face, says, "Fuck you!" Then he goes up to the next pirate, says, "Fuck you!" Then he does it to the next. After he finishes fuck you-ing each of the pirates, he says, "You have destroyed The World's Largest Watermelon and you must pay. Gimme two thousand dollars. Visa and Mastercard accepted."

Jolly Jill Rotgut takes off her flaming hat, threatens Jimbo Jim by holding it to his left ear. His ear hairs begin to crackle. He shrieks. Jolly Jill says, "Repeat after me: The crew of the Shoddy Barnacle are not responsible for any damages to the World's Largest Watermelon."

"The crew of the Shoddy Barnacle are not responsible for any damages to the World's Largest Watermelon."

"They do not need to pay me two thousand dollars."

"They do not need to pay me two thousand dollars."

"I will bring them to the body of Jesus."

"I will bring them to the body of Je…Wait a minute! I don't know where Jesus was buried. And he's probably a skeleton by now. But why do you need the body of Jesus? Jesus is inside us all. All you gotta do is flex and Jesus' muscle will pop out of your arm and fill you with love."

"Do you have a hippy-looking corpse that never decomposes?"

"Oh."

CHAPTER 44

Apocalypse Ninja enters the tent of Zeus, The Immortal Corpse. He admires Zeus's long, brown hair. The corpse probably could have been a member of The Glam Toasters during their heyday. Then he notices two long nails sticking out of the wounds in Zeus's palms.

Jesus.

Zeus is Jesus.

And Jimbo Jim is a freakin' idiot.

Jimbo Jim, the freakin' idiot, has also put Jesus in a caveman costume. The costume is the only thing stopping Apocalypse Ninja from completing his mission—that and homophobia. He snarls at the costume, trying to work up the nerve to remove it. *Who cares about my stupid mission?* he thinks. The Clan of REALLY evil ninjas can go suck a fuck.

Whenever he is nervous, he lets out a tiny, harmless fart. Apocalypse Ninja is nervous.

Mist travels with the fart, escaping from his rectum. The mist forms the shape of his mother and father. His father chants, "Apocalypse Ninja, you must complete your destiny."

"Why should I do anything you say?" he asks. "You guys used to be such dicks to me."

His mother says, "You made a promise to your dying ninja clan, a promise that cannot be broken.

"Crap."

Apocalypse Ninja may have many faults, but his greatest fault is he always keeps his promises.

CHAPTER 45

Apocalypse Ninja reaches for Jesus's caveman outfit.

The pirates enter the tent. "Hands off!" Jolly Jill Rotgut says, holding her burning hat to Jimbo Jim's eyeball. "Or this scallywag is gonna need an eye patch and he won't be able to find any steady employment besides working on a pirate ship."

"Actually," Jimbo Jim says, "I'm my own boss, so my physical appearance doesn't matter. It may even be good for business."

She clutches his throat with her tongs, says, "Shut up! I'm trying to prey on his human compassion."

Apocalypse Ninja says, "I don't give a crap about this guy. Who the hell is he anyway? You should burn his eye. It would be funny."

Jolly Jill Rotgut has a hissy fit, throws Jimbo Jim on the ground, screams, "Skinna-ma-rinky-dinky-doo!" and attacks Apocalypse Ninja's face with her juicer. The rest of the crew charge, ganging up on him: giving him a dead arm with an erect penis, cutting his neck open with a tiny plastic knife, making scary faces at him, tickling his feet.

Apocalypse Ninja totally gets his ass kicked.

CHAPTER 46

Apocalypse Ninja lies on the ground next to Jimbo Jim—bleeding, crying, bathing in his own urine—while the crew of the Shoddy Barnacle kick him all over with their pirate boots. He yells, "Stop it! Just stop it!" like a sissy girl. Then he is surprised when he feels the power of the ninja inside.

It surges through him. "It" being everything his teachers tried to teach in REALLY evil ninja school. *Tried* to teach him rather than *succeeded* at teaching him because he was too busy sleeping. REALLY evil ninja school was REALLY boring.

Apocalypse Ninja says, "Osmosis," becomes translucent, moonwalks through Fucking Pussy's body, solidifies in its center.

Fucking Pussy's body explodes. Apocalypse Ninja's Glam Toasters t-shirt is coated in blood, arteries.

Jolly Jill Rotgut says, "Holy mackerel!" She gapes at the remains of Fucking Pussy, says, "He was a pacifist! Why did you have to do that?"

Apocalypse Ninja says, "His scary faces were very scary," shoots lighting out of his fingertips. Manny gets hit, becomes unconscious.

Erection attacks. Apocalypse Ninja turns invisible, uses his REALLY evil ninja fighting skills. The pirate ends up hyperventilating on the floor. Apocalypse Ninja reappears, says, "HAHAHA! I am supreme!"

Terrified, Cracker flies away. But Apocalypse Ninja leaps against the side of the tent, ricochets skyward toward the parrot, dropkicks him in the face. Cracker falls, splats, says, "Petey doesn't want to die," and does just that.

Apocalypse Ninja turns to Jolly Jill Rotgut. She returns his gaze, weeping for her dead and fallen crewmembers.

Unhappy about what is happening, Jimbo Jim continues to lie on the ground.

CHAPTER 47

Jolly Jill Rotgut claws at Apocalypse Ninja's face with one tong, shoves the other down his throat, choking him.

He pushes her away, says, "Stop! I don't want to fight you. I can't hit a woman."

She is incredulous, says, "You can't hit a woman? What about back at the state fair? When you destroyed my face with a piece of wood? Remember *that*?"

"I don't know, man. Ever since I got these abilities to totally beat your ass, I've been really against violence toward women and shit, so can you just lay off so I can..." he makes a sour face, "...suck this guy's dick?"

Jolly Jill Rotgut gets angry. She picks up Apocalypse Ninja's extra extra extra extra extra large t-shirt, ties it around his throat in a tricky, tight pirate knot. He gasps for air. She points at his genitalia, snickers, pulls the extra extra large t-shirt. Pulls and pulls and pulls. She pulls so hard that she loses her grasp and Apocalypse Ninja falls onto the floor. He takes advantage of this by crawling over to Jesus Christ and pulling off his caveman costume.

Jesus Christ has a very large penis. Apocalypse Ninja stares at it, gasps, "Ass. Titties. Ass. Ass. Titties. Apocalypse Ninja loves the hoes!" He opens his mouth, goes in for the plunge.

CHAPTER 48

Erection scurries under Apocalypse Ninja's legs and does a handstand, shoving his medical condition into the ninja's mouth.

CHAPTER 49

Apocalypse Ninja tries to say, "Yucko!" but the pirate penis in his mouth makes it sound more like "oooooo."

Erection's erection wilts. A voice says, "Rest easy, my son. Your affliction is at its end."

Apocalypse Ninja thrusts his head back to get a better view. He sees Jesus Christ, awakened—wearing a tuxedo shirt and a pair of overalls—giving Erection a back massage. The pirate looks serene.

"Greetings and good tidings, Apocalypse Ninja."

"Whatever, man," he wheezes, getting down on his knees and scurrying toward Jesus's lap. "I made a promise to my dying ninja clan and I never break my promises."

Jesus stops massaging, unties Jolly Jill Rotgut's tricky, tight pirate knot, puts his hand on Apocalypse Ninja's brow, says, "Peace."

Apocalypse Ninja feels a deep sense of relaxation.

CHAPTER 50

Jesus says, "I know you do not want to make me come. It is ok to be yourself. It is ok to be uncomfortable around gay people and disgusted by the idea of performing fellatio if being uncomfortable and disgusted is your true nature. I am The Christ, your Lord and God, so I am comfortable around gay people and delighted when I am performing fellatio. But my subjects should not do as I do." Jesus starts to give Apocalypse Ninja a back massage. "It is also ok to break promises to your dying ninja clan when they involve bringing about the apocalypse. My son, you are absolved."

Apocalypse Ninja experiences bliss and knows his mission is over.

CHAPTER 51

And Jesus raises Fucking Pussy from the dead and heals his wounds. And Jolly Jill Rotgut sayeths, "Please bring my parrot back to life," and Jesus sayeths, "I cannot bring birds back to life, for they have no souls." And tears fall down Jolly Jill Rotgut's scarred cheeks. And Jesus rubs her temples while saying, "Facial facial facial" in a squeaky voice. And Jolly Jill Rotgut experiences joy. And Jesus sayeths, Let us have a dance party. And Apocalypse Ninja high-fives Jolly Jill Rotgut because high-fives are the holiest of holies. And Jesus hires The Glam Toasters and they play their greatest hits. And Jimbo Jim gets off the ground and happiness fills his chest. And Jesus sends party invitations to Apocalypse Ninja's parents, The Clan of REALLY Evil Ninjas, the anal re-tentive airport security guard, Scarlett Johansson, the beautiful redhead, Arnold Schwarzenegger and her stewardesses, the gas station attendant who did not appreciate being called a nigga, the gun store owner, the police officers who the pirates murdered, the police officers who the pirates did not murder, the man with the cowboy hat, Mysterio the Moving Cave, the man with the funny shorts, and the three-breasted women in bikinis. And they all arrive with smiles on their faces. And Jesus gives Manny a foot massage. And Jolly Jill Rotgut sayeths to Manny, "Oh my God! Who are you? You're so cute! Would you like to dance?" And the bodies of the partygoers part until Apocalypse Ninja is in the center of a circle. And Apocalypse Ninja does The Running Man. And everyone cheers because it was the greatest exhibition of The Running Man they have ever seen. And they dance and they dance until the end of the world.

EPILOGUE

Someone knocks on my door. I look out the peephole. Frankie Nougat waits in the hallway. I am disappointed that he has not been cut in half. I am even more disappointed that he is not Günter, my arms dealer who I have been expecting. Sometimes a man cannot fight the urge to feel the cold metal of a new semi-automatic weapon in his hands.

Frankie walks into my apartment. He tells me he's solved the case and I owe him six dollar for three days worth of detective work plus twelve dollars for expenses.

"Expenses?" I ask. "How could there possibly be any expenses? All you did was read three novellas."

"For ice cream," the junior detective says, "It helps me think. I have trouble using my junior detective skills unless I'm eating it."

"Fine," I say, "but I'm not paying you until you tell me the theme of my novel."

I lead him to my giraffe-skinned couch.

We're halfway there when a giant fist smashes through a wall and almost hits us. A grotesque face peeks in through the hole. It looks like a monstrous version of Monty Cantsin. "Want Donner Burger and fries now, Bradley!"

Frankie shivers with fear. "Isn't that Monty Cantsin?" he asks.

"Nah, that's just my neighbor. Don't worry about him." I rub the junior detective's shoulders to calm the boy down, "He does this every once in a while. Pretends he's the Incredible Hulk. No big deal. I've gotten used to it."

We both sit on my couch. "So tell me what you've found out," I say.

"Well, the theme of "Apocalypse Ninja" is exploitation. You tried to exploit the pirates vs. ninjas meme in an attempt to become wealthier than J.K. Rowling but failed horribly because you were unable to write a novel that was long enough to deserve its own book. So I guess the novella has two themes: exploitation AND failure."

Anger scars my face. I reach for Frankie's throat.

Apocalypse Ninja crashes through my window ass-first. The crew of the Shoddy Barnacle break down my door. They rush toward Apocalypse Ninja. He tries to go back outside, but is unable to fit through the window. Jolly Jill Rotgut pokes one of her tongs up Apocalypse Ninja's anus. He squeals. The rest of the crew approach their captain, prepared to assist her.

"Want Donner Burger and Fries!" yells the giant version of Monty.

"Listen, guys," I say, turning to Monty and then to the pirates. "Can you just give this detective kid and I a few minutes of peace so I can wring the truth out of him?"

Monty and the pirates nod, pause, wait patiently for the grand revelation.

"Hey, Frankie. There is no way the themes of this novel are exploitation and failure. 'Apocalypse Ninja' has absolutely nothing to do with those things and they're even less relevant to the other two novels."

I wait with my arms inches away from Frankie's ability to continue to breathe.

Frankie says, "Alright, Mr. Sands, I have discovered the true theme of *Please Do Not Shoot Me in the Face*: it concerns the acceptance of Jesus as our lord and savior. If the readers of this book had accepted Jesus before reading the novella about me, he wouldn't have stolen anyone's heart. He would have had better things to do in 'Cheesequake Smash-Up' than decide the winner of a demolition derby, like enforcing world peace. He probably wouldn't have made the NGA Building the winner since it sort of popularized cannibalism around the world and it is not very Christian to eat your fellow man. Well, unless you're eating Jesus, but there's not enough of him to go around. As for 'Apocalypse Ninja,' it's the stupidest thing anyone has ever written."

Hey!

"If your readers had accepted Jesus as their Lord and Savior they would have never read it and you would have been saved from the shame that will haunt you for the rest of your life. A fat, useless ninja seeks out Jesus so he can bring about the end of the world by doing naughty things to his pee-pee? Where do you come up with this trash, Mr. Sands? Aren't you embarrassed?"

No, I'm not embarrassed that I've written one of the three greatest novellas of the twenty-first century. But what's with this crap about the theme of my novel being the acceptance of Jesus as our Lord and Savior? I have never been so pissed off in my life. I wish Günter would get his ass over here so I could convert my internal rage into external rage.

"But *Please Do Not Shoot Me in the Face* is still a very important book, Mr. Sands. It doesn't matter if it's a collection of novellas or a novel. Like the *Bible*, it is a collection of stories that varies significantly from one another. And no one ever wonders if the *Bible* is a novel or a collection stories. It is what it is: the most important book of our civilization."

I stop wanting to murder Frankie and give him a big hug. *Please Do Not Shoot Me in the Face* was going to be as important as the *Bible*. More important even. And I was going to be richer than God.

Overjoyed, I attempt to breakdance although I have never done it before in my life. It really hurt, but I don't care.

Richer than God.

A knock on my door interrupts my dancing. It is a delightful reprieve from my pain. I answer the door. It is Günter. I hurry him inside, anxious to feel the cold metal of a new semi-automatic weapon in his hands. He hands me a gun. I reach for it and Günter's elbow accidently brushes against the trigger.

There is a loud discharge. I lie on the floor of my apartment, blood pouring over my eyeballs. The center of my head feels funny, as if it is a foot rather than a head and my foot-head has fallen asleep.

As I mourn my life, I regret never telling Günter the name of my current novel. He asked me last time we made a transaction, but I kept quiet, fearing he would steal the title for one of the action movies he makes in his spare time.

I die. And as I die, my characters die with me.

ABOUT THE AUTHOR

Bradley Sands it the author of *Rico Slade Will Fucking Kill You, Sorry I Ruined Your Orgy*, and other books. His work has appeared in *Warmed and Bound*, *The Magazine of Bizarro Fiction*, *Nouns of Assemblage*, Word Riot, *No Colony*, Lamination Colony, and many other places in print and online. Bradley is also the editor of the fiction journal *Bust Down the Door and Eat All the Chickens*.

Visit him online at www.bradleysands.com.

Bizarro book

CATALOG   SPRING 201

Bizarro Books publishes under the following imprints:

www.rawdogscreamingpress.com

www.eraserheadpress.co

www.afterbirthbooks.com

www.swallowdownpress.c

For all your Bizarro needs visit:

WWW.BIZARROCENTRAL.COM

Introduce yourselves to the bizarro fiction genre and all of its authors with the Bizarro Starter Kit series. Each volume features short novels and short stories by ten of the leading bizarro authors, designed to give you a perfect sampling of the genre for only $10.

BB-0X1
"The Bizarro Starter Kit"
(Orange)
Featuring D. Harlan Wilson, Carlton Mellick III, Jeremy Robert Johnson, Kevin L Donihe, Gina Ranalli, Andre Duza, Vincent W. Sakowski, Steve Beard, John Edward Lawson, and Bruce Taylor.
236 pages $10

BB-0X2
"The Bizarro Starter Kit"
(Blue)
Featuring Ray Fracalossy, Jeremy C. Shipp, Jordan Krall, Mykle Hansen, Andersen Prunty, Eckhard Gerdes, Bradley Sands, Steve Aylett, Christian TeBordo, and Tony Rauch. **244 pages $10**

BB-0X2
"The Bizarro Starter Kit"
(Purple)
Featuring Russell Edson, Athena Villaverde, David Agranoff, Matthew Revert, Andrew Goldfarb, Jeff Burk, Garrett Cook, Kris Saknussemm, Cody Goodfellow, and Cameron Pierce **264 pages $10**

BB-001 "The Kafka Effekt" D. Harlan Wilson — A collection of forty-four irreal short stories loosely written in the vein of Franz Kafka, with more than a pinch of William S. Burroughs sprinkled on top. **211 pages $14**

BB-002 "Satan Burger" Carlton Mellick III — The cult novel that put Carlton Mellick III on the map ... Six punks get jobs at a fast food restaurant owned by the devil in a city violently overpopulated by surreal alien cultures. **236 pages $14**

BB-003 "Some Things Are Better Left Unplugged" Vincent Sakwoski — Join The Man and his Nemesis, the obese tabby, for a nightmare roller coaster ride into this postmodern fantasy. **152 pages $10**

BB-004 "Shall We Gather At the Garden?" Kevin L Donihe — Donihe's Debut novel. Midgets take over the world, The Church of Lionel Richie vs. The Church of the Byrds, plant porn and more! **244 pages $14**

BB-005 "Razor Wire Pubic Hair" Carlton Mellick III — A genderless humandildo is purchased by a razor dominatrix and brought into her nightmarish world of bizarre sex and mutilation. **176 pages $11**

BB-006 "Stranger on the Loose" D. Harlan Wilson — The fiction of Wilson's 2nd collection is planted in the soil of normalcy, but what grows out of that soil is a dark, witty, otherworldly jungle... **228 pages $14**

BB-007 "The Baby Jesus Butt Plug" Carlton Mellick III — Using clones of the Baby Jesus for anal sex will be the hip sex fetish of the future. **92 pages $10**

BB-008 "Fishyfleshed" Carlton Mellick III — The world of the past is an illogical flatland lacking in dimension and color, a sick-scape of crispy squid people wandering the desert for no apparent reason. **260 pages $14**

BB-009 "Dead Bitch Army" Andre Duza — Step into a world filled with racist teenagers, cannibals, 100 warped Uncle Sams, automobiles with razor-sharp teeth, living graffiti, and a pissed-off zombie bitch out for revenge. **344 pages $16**

BB-010 "The Menstruating Mall" Carlton Mellick III — "The Breakfast Club meets Chopping Mall as directed by David Lynch." - Brian Keene **212 pages $12**

BB-011 "Angel Dust Apocalypse" Jeremy Robert Johnson — Meth-heads, man-made monsters, and murderous Neo-Nazis. "Seriously amazing short stories..." - Chuck Palahniuk, author of Fight Club **184 pages $11**

BB-012 "Ocean of Lard" Kevin L Donihe / Carlton Mellick III — A parody of those old Choose Your Own Adventure kid's books about some very odd pirates sailing on a sea made of animal fat. **176 pages $12**

BB-015 "Foop!" Chris Genoa — Strange happenings are going on at Dactyl, Inc, the world's first and only time travel tourism company.
"A surreal pie in the face!" - Christopher Moore **300 pages $14**

BB-020 "Punk Land" Carlton Mellick III — In the punk version of Heaven, the anarchist utopia is threatened by corporate fascism and only Goblin, Mortician's sperm, and a blue-mohawked female assassin named Shark Girl can stop them. **284 pages $15**

BB-027 "Siren Promised" Jeremy Robert Johnson & Alan M Clark — Nominated for the Bram Stoker Award. A potent mix of bad drugs, bad dreams, brutal bad guys, and surreal/incredible art by Alan M. Clark. **190 pages $13**

BB-031"Sea of the Patchwork Cats" Carlton Mellick III — A quiet dreamlike tale set in the ashes of the human race. For Mellick enthusiasts who also adore The Twilight Zone. **112 pages $10**

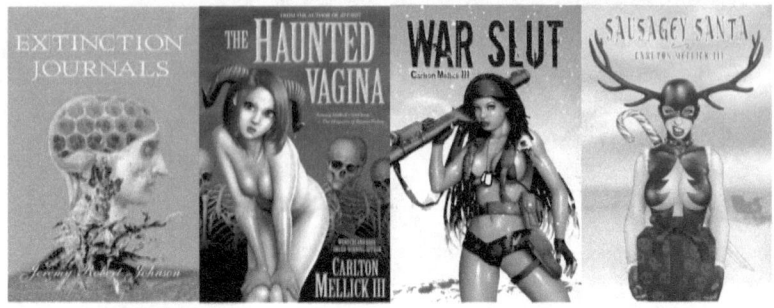

BB-032 **"Extinction Journals" Jeremy Robert Johnson** — An uncanny voyage across a newly nuclear America where one man must confront the problems associated with loneliness, insane dieties, radiation, love, and an ever-evolving cockroach suit with a mind of its own. **104 pages $10**

BB-037 **"The Haunted Vagina" Carlton Mellick III** — It's difficult to love a woman whose vagina is a gateway to the world of the dead. **132 pages $10**

BB-043 **"War Slut" Carlton Mellick III** — Part "1984," part "Waiting for Godot," and part action horror video game adaptation of John Carpenter's "The Thing." **116 pages $10**

BB-047 **"Sausagey Santa" Carlton Mellick III** — A bizarro Christmas tale featuring Santa as a piratey mutant with a body made of sausages. 124 pages $10

BB-048 **"Misadventures in a Thumbnail Universe" Vincent Sakowski** — Dive deep into the surreal and satirical realms of neo-classical Blender Fiction, filled with television shoes and flesh-filled skies. **120 pages $10**

BB-053 **"Ballad of a Slow Poisoner" Andrew Goldfarb** — Millford Mutterwurst sat down on a Tuesday to take his afternoon tea, and made the unpleasant discovery that his elbows were becoming flatter. **128 pages $10**

BB-055 **"Help! A Bear is Eating Me" Mykle Hansen** — The bizarro, heartwarming, magical tale of poor planning, hubris and severe blood loss...
150 pages $11

BB-056 **"Piecemeal June" Jordan Krall** — A man falls in love with a living sex doll, but with love comes danger when her creator comes after her with crab-squid assassins. **90 pages $9**

BB-058 "The Overwhelming Urge" Andersen Prunty — A collection of bizarro tales by Andersen Prunty. **150 pages $11**

BB-059 "Adolf in Wonderland" Carlton Mellick III — A dreamlike adventure that takes a young descendant of Adolf Hitler's design and sends him down the rabbit hole into a world of imperfection and disorder. **180 pages $11**

BB-061 "Ultra Fuckers" Carlton Mellick III — Absurdist suburban horror about a couple who enter an upper middle class gated community but can't find their way out. **108 pages $9**

BB-062 "House of Houses" Kevin L. Donihe — An odd man wants to marry his house. Unfortunately, all of the houses in the world collapse at the same time in the Great House Holocaust. Now he must travel to House Heaven to find his departed fiancee. **172 pages $11**

BB-064 "Squid Pulp Blues" Jordan Krall — In these three bizarro-noir novellas, the reader is thrown into a world of murderers, drugs made from squid parts, deformed gun-toting veterans, and a mischievous apocalyptic donkey. **204 pages $12**

BB-065 "Jack and Mr. Grin" Andersen Prunty — "When Mr. Grin calls you can hear a smile in his voice. Not a warm and friendly smile, but the kind that seizes your spine in fear. You don't need to pay your phone bill to hear it. That smile is in every line of Prunty's prose." - Tom Bradley. **208 pages $12**

BB-066 "Cybernetrix" Carlton Mellick III — What would you do if your normal everyday world was slowly mutating into the video game world from Tron? **212 pages $12**

BB-072 "Zerostrata" Andersen Prunty — Hansel Nothing lives in a tree house, suffers from memory loss, has a very eccentric family, and falls in love with a woman who runs naked through the woods every night. **144 pages $11**

BB-073 "The Egg Man" Carlton Mellick III — It is a world where humans reproduce like insects. Children are the property of corporations, and having an enormous ten-foot brain implanted into your skull is a grotesque sexual fetish. Mellick's industrial urban dystopia is one of his darkest and grittiest to date. **184 pages $11**

BB-074 "Shark Hunting in Paradise Garden" Cameron Pierce — A group of strange humanoid religious fanatics travel back in time to the Garden of Eden to discover it is invested with hundreds of giant flying maneating sharks. **150 pages $10**

BB-075 "Apeshit" Carlton Mellick III - Friday the 13th meets Visitor Q. Six hipster teens go to a cabin in the woods inhabited by a deformed killer. An incredibly fucked-up parody of B-horror movies with a bizarro slant. **192 pages $12**

BB-076 "Fuckers of Everything on the Crazy Shitting Planet of the Vomit At smosphere" Mykle Hansen - Three bizarro satires. Monster Cocks, Journey to the Center of Agnes Cuddlebottom, and Crazy Shitting Planet. **228 pages $12**

BB-077 "The Kissing Bug" Daniel Scott Buck — In the tradition of Roald Dahl, Tim Burton, and Edward Gorey, comes this bizarro anti-war children's story about a bohemian conenose kissing bug who falls in love with a human woman. **116 pages $10**

BB-078 "MachoPoni" Lotus Rose — It's My Little Pony... *Bizarro* style! A long time ago Poniworld was split in two. On one side of the Jagged Line is the Pastel Kingdom, a magical land of music, parties, and positivity. On the other side of the Jagged Line is Dark Kingdom inhabited by an army of undead ponies. **148 pages $11**

BB-079 "The Faggiest Vampire" Carlton Mellick III — A Roald Dahl-esque children's story about two faggy vampires who partake in a mustache competition to find out which one is truly the faggiest. **104 pages $10**

BB-080 "Sky Tongues" Gina Ranalli — The autobiography of Sky Tongues, the biracial hermaphrodite actress with tongues for fingers. Follow her strange life story as she rises from freak to fame. **204 pages $12**

BB-081 **"Washer Mouth" Kevin L. Donihe** - A washing machine becomes human and pursues his dream of meeting his favorite soap opera star. **244 pages $11**

BB-082 **"Shatnerquake" Jeff Burk** - All of the characters ever played by William Shatner are suddenly sucked into our world. Their mission: hunt down and destroy the real William Shatner. **100 pages $10**

BB-083 **"The Cannibals of Candyland" Carlton Mellick III** - There exists a race of cannibals that are made of candy. They live in an underground world made out of candy. One man has dedicated his life to killing them all. **170 pages $11**

BB-084 **"Slub Glub in the Weird World of the Weeping Willows"** **Andrew Goldfarb** - The charming tale of a blue glob named Slub Glub who helps the weeping willows whose tears are flooding the earth. There are also hyenas, ghosts, and a voodoo priest **100 pages $10**

BB-085 **"Super Fetus" Adam Pepper** - Try to abort this fetus and he'll kick your ass! **104 pages $10**

BB-086 **"Fistful of Feet" Jordan Krall** - A bizarro tribute to spaghetti westerns, featuring Cthulhu-worshipping Indians, a woman with four feet, a crazed gunman who is obsessed with sucking on candy, Syphilis-ridden mutants, sexually transmitted tattoos, and a house devoted to the freakiest fetishes. **228 pages $12**

BB-087 **"Ass Goblins of Auschwitz" Cameron Pierce** - It's Monty Python meets Nazi exploitation in a surreal nightmare as can only be imagined by Bizarro author Cameron Pierce. **104 pages $10**

BB-088 **"Silent Weapons for Quiet Wars" Cody Goodfellow** - "This is high-end psychological surrealist horror meets bottom-feeding low-life crime in a techno-thrilling science fiction world full of Lovecraft and magic..." -John Skipp **212 pages $12**

BB-089 **"Warrior Wolf Women of the Wasteland" Carlton Mellick III**
— Road Warrior Werewolves versus McDonaldland Mutants...post-apocalyptic fiction has never been quite like this. **316 pages $13**

BB-091 **"Super Giant Monster Time" Jeff Burk** — A tribute to choose your own adventures and Godzilla movies. Will you escape the giant monsters that are rampaging the fuck out of your city and shit? Or will you join the mob of alien-controlled punk rockers causing chaos in the streets? What happens next depends on you. **188 pages $12**

BB-092 **"Perfect Union" Cody Goodfellow** — "Cronenberg's THE FLY on a grand scale: human/insect gene-spliced body horror, where the human hive politics are as shocking as the gore." -John Skipp. **272 pages $13**

BB-093 **"Sunset with a Beard" Carlton Mellick III** — 14 stories of surreal science fiction. **200 pages $12**

BB-094 **"My Fake War" Andersen Prunty** — The absurd tale of an unlikely soldier forced to fight a war that, quite possibly, does not exist. It's Rambo meets Waiting for Godot in this subversive satire of American values and the scope of the human imagination. **128 pages $11**

BB-095 **"Lost in Cat Brain Land" Cameron Pierce** — Sad stories from a surreal world. A fascist mustache, the ghost of Franz Kafka, a desert inside a dead cat. Primordial entities mourn the death of their child. The desperate serve tea to mysterious creatures. A hopeless romantic falls in love with a pterodactyl. And much more. **152 pages $11**

BB-096 **"The Kobold Wizard's Dildo of Enlightenment +2" Carlton Mellick III** — A Dungeons and Dragons parody about a group of people who learn they are only made up characters in an AD&D campaign and must find a way to resist their nerdy teenaged players and retarded dungeon master in order to survive. 232 **pages $12**

BB-098 **"A Hundred Horrible Sorrows of Ogner Stump" Andrew Goldfarb** — Goldfarb's acclaimed comic series. A magical and weird journey into the horrors of everyday life. **164 pages $11**

BB-099 **"Pickled Apocalypse of Pancake Island" Cameron Pierce**—A demented fairy tale about a pickle, a pancake, and the apocalypse. **102 pages $8**

BB-100 **"Slag Attack" Andersen Prunty**— Slag Attack features four visceral, noir stories about the living, crawling apocalypse.A slag is what survivors are calling the slug-like maggots raining from the sky, burrowing inside people, and hollowing out their flesh and their sanity. **148 pages $11**

BB-101 **"Slaughterhouse High" Robert Devereaux**—A place where schools are built with secret passageways, rebellious teens get zippers installed in their mouths and genitals, and once a year, on that special night, one couple is slaughtered and the bits of their bodies are kept as souvenirs. **304 pages $13**

BB-102 **"The Emerald Burrito of Oz" John Skipp & Marc Levinthal** —OZ IS REAL! Magic is real! The gate is really in Kansas! And America is finally allowing Earth tourists to visit this weird-ass, mysterious land. But when Gene of Los Angeles heads off for summer vacation in the Emerald City, little does he know that a war is brewing...a war that could destroy both worlds. **280 pages $13**

BB-103 **"The Vegan Revolution... with Zombies" David Agranoff** — When there's no more meat in hell, the vegans will walk the earth. **160 pages $11**

BB-104 **"The Flappy Parts" Kevin L Donihe**—Poems about bunnies, LSD, and police abuse. You know, things that matter. 132 **pages $11**

BB-105 **"Sorry I Ruined Your Orgy" Bradley Sands**—Bizarro humorist Bradley Sands returns with one of the strangest, most hilarious collections of the year. **130 pages $11**

BB-106 **"Mr. Magic Realism" Bruce Taylor**—Like Golden Age science fiction comics written by Freud, *Mr. Magic Realism* is a strange, insightful adventure that spans the furthest reaches of the galaxy, exploring the hidden caverns in the hearts and minds of men, women, aliens, and biomechanical cats. **152 pages $11**

BB-107 **"Zombies and Shit" Carlton Mellick III**—"Battle Royale" meets "Return of the Living Dead." Mellick's bizarro tribute to the zombie genre. **308 pages $13**

BB-108 **"The Cannibal's Guide to Ethical Living" Mykle Hansen**— Over a five star French meal of fine wine, organic vegetables and human flesh, a lunatic delivers a witty, chilling, disturbingly sane argument in favor of eating the rich.. **184 pages $11**

BB-109 **"Starfish Girl" Athena Villaverde**—In a post-apocalyptic underwater dome society, a girl with a starfish growing from her head and an assassin with sea anenome hair are on the run from a gang of mutant fish men. **160 pages $11**

BB-110 **"Lick Your Neighbor" Chris Genoa**—Mutant ninjas, a talking whale, kung fu masters, maniacal pilgrims, and an alcoholic clown populate Chris Genoa's surreal, darkly comical and unnerving reimagining of the first Thanksgiving. **303 pages $13**

BB-111 **"Night of the Assholes" Kevin L. Donihe**—A plague of assholes is infecting the countryside. Normal everyday people are transforming into jerks, snobs, dicks, and douchebags. And they all have only one purpose: to make your life a living hell.. **192 pages $11**

BB-112 **"Jimmy Plush, Teddy Bear Detective" Garrett Cook**—Hard-boiled cases of a private detective trapped within a teddy bear body. **180 pages $11**

BB-113 **"The Deadheart Shelters" Forrest Armstrong**—The hip hop lovechild of William Burroughs and Dali... **144 pages $11**

BB-114 **"Eyeballs Growing All Over Me... Again" Tony Raugh**— Absurd, surreal, playful, dream-like, whimsical, and a lot of fun to read. **144 pages $11**

BB-115 **"Whargoul" Dave Brockie** — From the killing grounds of Stalingrad to the death camps of the holocaust. From torture chambers in Iraq to race riots in the United States, the Whargoul was there, killing and raping. **244 pages $12**

BB-116 **"By the Time We Leave Here, We'll Be Friends" J. David Osborne** — A David Lynchian nightmare set in a Russian gulag, where its prisoners, guards, traitors, soldiers, lovers, and demons fight for survival and their own rapidly deteriorating humanity. **168 pages $11**

BB-117 **"Christmas on Crack" edited by Carlton Mellick III** — Perverted Christmas Tales for the whole family! . . . as long as every member of your family is over the age of 18. **168 pages $11**

BB-118 **"Crab Town" Carlton Mellick III** — Radiation fetishists, balloon people, mutant crabs, sail-bike road warriors, and a love affair between a woman and an H-Bomb. This is one mean asshole of a city. Welcome to Crab Town. **100 pages $8**

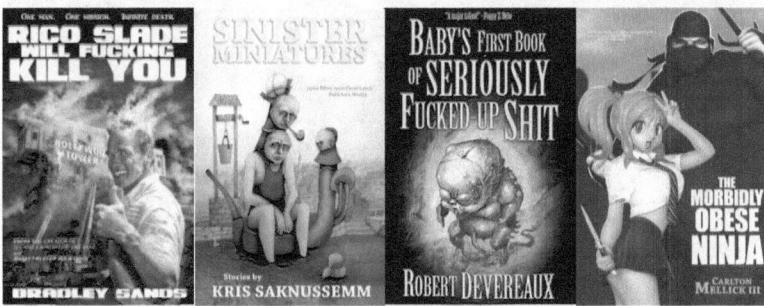

BB-119 **"Rico Slade Will Fucking Kill You" Bradley Sands** — Rico Slade is an action hero. Rico Slade can rip out a throat with his bare hands. Rico Slade's favorite food is the honey-roasted peanut. Rico Slade will fucking kill everyone. A novel. **122 pages $8**

BB-120 **"Sinister Miniatures" Kris Saknussemm** — The definitive collection of short fiction by Kris Saknussemm, confirming that he is one of the best, most daring writers of the weird to emerge in the twenty-first century. **180 pages $11**

BB-121 **"Baby's First Book of Seriously Fucked up Shit" Robert Devereaux** — Ten stories of the strange, the gross, and the just plain fucked up from one of the most original voices in horror. **176 pages $11**

BB-122 **"The Morbidly Obese Ninja" Carlton Mellick III** — These days, if you want to run a successful company . . . you're going to need a lot of ninjas. **92 pages $8**

BB-123 **"Abortion Arcade" Cameron Pierce** — An intoxicating blend of body horror and midnight movie madness, reminiscent of early David Lynch and the splatterpunks at their most sublime. **172 pages $11**

BB-124 **"Black Hole Blues" Patrick Wensink** — A hilarious double helix of country music and physics. **196 pages $11**

BB-125 **"Barbarian Beast Bitches of the Badlands" Carlton Mellick III** — Three prequels and sequels to *Warrior Wolf Women of the Wasteland.* **284 pages $13**

BB-126 **"The Traveling Dildo Salesman" Kevin L. Donihe** — A nightmare comedy about destiny, faith, and sex toys. Also featuring Donihe's most lurid and infamous short stories: *Milky Agitation, Two-Way Santa, The Helen Mower, Living Room Zombies,* and *Revenge of the Living Masturbation Rag.* **108 pages $8**

BB-127 **"Metamorphosis Blues" Bruce Taylor** — Enter a land of love beasts, intergalactic cowboys, and rock 'n roll. A land where Sears Catalogs are doorways to insanity and men keep mysterious black boxes. Welcome to the monstrous mind of Mr. Magic Realism. **136 pages $11**

BB-128 **"The Driver's Guide to Hitting Pedestrians" Andersen Prunty** — A pocket guide to the twenty-three most painful things in life, written by the most well-adjusted man in the universe. **108 pages $8**

BB-129 **"Island of the Super People" Kevin Shamel** — Four students and their anthropology professor journey to a remote island to study its indigenous population. But this is no ordinary native culture. They're super heroes and villains with flesh costumes and out-landish abilities like self-detonation, musical eyelashes, and microwave hands. **194 pages $11**

BB-130 **"Fantastic Orgy" Carlton Mellick III** — Shark Sex, mutant cats, and strange sexually transmitted diseases. Featuring the stories: *Candy-coated, Ear Cat, Fantastic Orgy, City Hobgoblins,* and *Porno in August.* **136 pages $9**

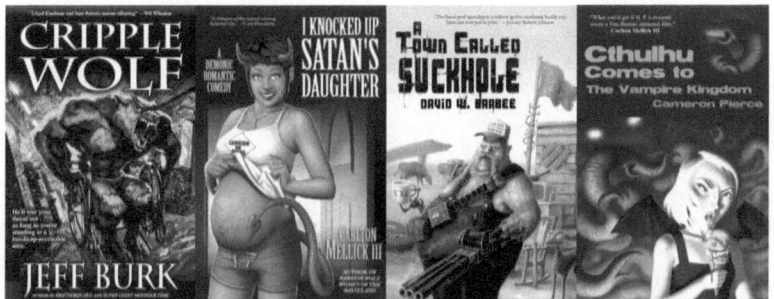

BB-131 **"Cripple Wolf" Jeff Burk** — Part man. Part wolf. 100% crippled. Also including *Punk Rock Nursing Home, Adrift with Space Badgers, Cook for Your Life, Just Another Day in the Park, Frosty and the Full Monty,* and *House of Cats.* **152 pages $10**

BB-132 **"I Knocked Up Satan's Daughter" Carlton Mellick III** — An adorable, violent, fantastical love story. A romantic comedy for the bizarro fiction reader. **152 pages $10**

BB-133 **"A Town Called Suckhole" David W. Barbee** — Far into the future, in the nuclear bowels of post-apocalyptic Dixie, there is a town. A town of derelict mobile homes, ancient junk, and mutant wildlife. A town of slack jawed rednecks who bask in the splendors of moonshine and mud boggin'. A town dedicated to the bloody and demented legacy of the Old South. A town called Suckhole. **144 pages $10**

BB-134 **"Cthulhu Comes to the Vampire Kingdom" Cameron Pierce** — What you'd get if H. P. Lovecraft wrote a Tim Burton animated film. **148 pages $11**

BB-135 **"I am Genghis Cum" Violet LeVoit** — From the savage Arctic tundra to post-partum mutations to your missing daughter's unmarked grave, join visionary madwoman Violet LeVoit in this non-stop eight-story onslaught of full-tilt Bizarro punk lit thrills. **124 pages $9**

BB-136 **"Haunt" Laura Lee Bahr** — A tripping-balls Los Angeles noir, where a mysterious dame drags you through a time-warping Bizarro hall of mirrors. **316 pages $13**

BB-137 **"Amazing Stories of the Flying Spaghetti Monster" edited by Cameron Pierce** — Like an all-spaghetti evening of Adult Swim, the Flying Spaghetti Monster will show you the many realms of His Noodly Appendage. Learn of those who worship him and the lives he touches in distant, mysterious ways. **228 pages $12**

BB-138 **"Wave of Mutilation" Douglas Lain** — A dream-pop exploration of modern architecture and the American identity, *Wave of Mutilation* is a Zen finger trap for the 21st century. **100 pages $8**

www.ingramcontent.com/pod-product-compliance
Lightning Source LLC
Chambersburg PA
CBHW020837260626
47169CB00003B/1035